Destined
Hearts

Kate Allenton

Discover other titles by Kate Allenton

At

www.kateallenton.com

ISBN-13:
978-0692439692
ISBN-10:
0692439692

1 CHAPTER

Lily Bennett ushered her mother and father toward the front door of her newly purchased house. She was thirty minutes into the task of trying to get them to leave. With every step forward, they'd pause and come up with yet another reason why they thought she should move home.

"What if you get scared?" Emma Bennett asked her daughter.

"Then I'll grab my gun and call 911." She soothed her mother's arms. "Don't worry, mom. The things that go bump in the night no longer scare me. When they realized that I could see them, it took all of the fun out of their games. Honest." The gift of seeing ghosts that she'd inherited from her mother was now her curse. She'd never break the bonds, never be able to move on, not that she was ready to let go. The choice was no longer her own.

"But you aren't used to this house," her mom retorted. "What if it's infested with rats or something worse?"

Rats she could handle, the constant reminder in the form of a ghost was much harder.

"Then I'll call an exterminator. Mom, I'll be fine." Lily kissed her mother's cheek before entwining their arms, ushering them another step closer. Five more steps and she would be home free, able to go back to her quiet existence.

"What if there's a fire?" her dad, Jake Bennett, asked. Leave it to her good old dad to be thinking of the practical. As the owner of Tactical Maneuvers, he was all about security and safety.

"You're not helping," Lily said, through gritted teeth, while glancing over her shoulder toward the instigator. His eyes glinted with mischief while he tried to stifle a smile. Troublemaker.

"He's right. What if there's a fire?" Her mom worried.

"Then I'll put it out. I own a fire extinguisher." She held up her hand. "Gas and electrical, I have one of each. They're both up to code and so is this house. You and dad had it checked and rechecked. It's safe."

"What if the fire is too big?" her mom continued.

"Then I'll get out and call the fire department," Lily answered. "I'm twenty-five years old, and you guys are acting as though I'm twelve and have never lived alone."

"Honey, we're just worried. You've been through a traumatic experience."

Lily's heart clenched as she tried to chase away the memories that haunted her and the future that had been stripped away.

Emma shrugged out of Lily's hold and set her purse on the table in the foyer. "Fine, if you're not coming home, then I'm staying. Honey, go home and pack me a bag."

Lily turned toward her father, her eyes widened as she begged for help.

"Come on, Emma. We've got the place wired with security; she's armed, and the ghosts will keep her company. She'll be fine. Besides, if you get one of your inner PMS-like radar signals indicating a family member is in trouble, then we'll check here first. She'll be fine."

That was a gift that Lily was thankful she'd never received. The thought of having cramps, other than her time of the month, wasn't something she'd ever wish on anyone. Well, maybe an ex-boyfriend or two. Her mother's cramps were the start of the family phone tree, and that was how it had been for years. It was the first indicator that one of the family members was in trouble. No, thank you.

"But..."

"If she's old enough to buy all this land and a three-story house, then she's old enough to stay in it by herself."

"I knew we shouldn't have made her trust fund available until she was forty instead of twenty-five." Emma grumbled.

"She would have bought the place anyway with..." Her dad frowned and never finished the sentence.

Lily knew his unspoken words; they were something she'd not easily forget. Life insurance, she'd never asked for or even knew about. Lily pushed the thoughts away like hoping the heartache would go with it.

Her dad took her mom by the elbow and led her toward the door. He grabbed her purse and broke the threshold, finally getting the woman outside and on the porch. A nice hot bath and a glass of wine were in sight. "Come on, Emma. How about we take a nice drive through town and we'll check out the Christmas decorations. That always gets you in a better mood."

Emma pulled Lily into her arms and squeezed her tight. "We're just a phone call away if you need anything, anything at all."

"I know, Mom." Lily tried for a reassuring smile. "I love you."

"I love you too."

Her mom walked down the porch steps and got into the car, not waiting on Lily's father. "You're in for a lecture on the ride home."

Her dad tossed his arm around her shoulder and kissed her forehead like he'd done all of her life. "She means well. She's just worried about you."

"I know, Dad," Lily whispered. "I'll call her tomorrow."

"Lock up behind us."

"Would you stop, already?" Lily asked, already knowing the answer, her own personal way of acknowledging that he cared and loved her too.

"I'll never stop." He managed a smile before releasing her to walk out onto the porch. "Good night, kiddo."

"Good night, Dad." She waited at the door, waving as they drove out of sight.

She closed and locked the door before setting the alarm. One glance at all of the packing boxes stacked against the wall and she kept walking. The floorboards creaked with each step. The 1906-built home held secrets all right. She'd already caught a glimpse of one ghost without even going into the attic. She liked new buildings just because of her gift, yet this one had called to her soul, like a long-lost memory forgotten years ago. It held Southern charm. It was warm and inviting, and it was all hers, the second oldest house in Southall, North Carolina, only rivaled in age by one other, the one her Aunt Claire owned.

Lily walked into the kitchen and poured a much-needed glass of wine before heading upstairs. She ran her hand over the intricate design in the wood banister. The entire house was filled with hand-carved wood and well preserved through the ages. It was the first thing she'd noticed when the realtor showed her the house and the reason why she signed on the dotted line. The great deal she'd gotten was just icing on the cake.

Opening the door to the master suite, she let out a sigh of relief. Her room was the only one unpacked while the rest of the house lay in shambles. A problem for another day. She grabbed her robe and started a bath, pouring rose-scented bubbles under the stream before stripping out of her clothes. She grabbed her glass of wine and eased down into the scalding water, hoping it would ease her tired muscles and aches. Well, at least the aches she could control.

She took a sip of wine and set the glass on the rim of the tub. Closing her eyes, she let the floral fragrance surround her and seep into her bones. This was what she needed, what she'd been waiting for all day.

The room chilled around her shoulders, producing goose bumps on her ivory skin. If her eyes were open, she'd see frost in the air from her breath like every other night for the last six months. He was here. He was always here.

"You look tired." The sound of the familiar male voice made her heart ache, her rest and relaxation gone, like her parents.

Without even opening her eyes, she knew who she'd find. It was the same every night. Every day. No matter where she moved, no matter how far she ran, it didn't matter. He was with her. Always in her heart and in her mind, just not in the way she needed him most. In the flesh.

"That's because I am, so go away," she answered without opening her eyes. *Stay,* she pleaded in her mind, a plea he'd fulfill if she'd speak the words.

"You don't mean that." His voice felt like a caress against her skin.

Her eyes slid open, his ghostly presence a reminder of everything she'd lost that fateful night. "Hey you."

He grinned in greeting, like he'd done every night for the last six months. "Hey you," he echoed. "I like the house."

She picked up her wine and took another sip, letting the flavor of the white wine linger on her tongue. No amount of alcohol could make her forget. No amount could make things right. "Mmmm, me too."

She leaned back and closed her eyes. Seeing his face made her heart ache worse every night, like a fresh stab in the chest, an open wound she relived every day. "You know you can't stay."

"I'll stay as long as you need me."

She shook her head, biting back the sting of tears forming behind her eyes. If she opened her eyes, they'd roll down her face like the pebbles of water on her skin. She kept them closed and swallowed around the forming lump in her throat. "I don't need you," she lied. "It's time for you to go."

"Not yet, but soon. You weren't meant to be mine, I know that now. You'll love again."

Her eyes flew open, and for once, she let him see what his death was doing to her. How much she loved him. She knew; why didn't he? "It isn't in my cards. You were it for me. Your memory will be enough."

"My memory can't keep you warm. My memory can't hold you at night. You need more. You deserve more, and when that need is filled and your heart is mended and full, then I'll leave...for good."

The thought of never seeing his face had her rethinking all of the times she'd wished just for that. She was wrong. She needed him. His presence provided just a little comfort even with the pain.

"He's coming, Lily, whether you're ready or not. It's been written in the stars."

"I'll never love another," she ground out through gritted teeth. How could he think she'd ever be okay, that any of this would ever be right? Anger stirred as heat crept up her neck. He thought he knew her? Well, he was wrong. She picked up her wine glass and threw it across the room. She'd never allow another to get that close again.

"You will," he retorted, his voice dissipating like his body. The air in the room warmed, letting her know he'd left her again. Her shoulders trembled as she let the tears fall free like she did every night after his visit. She held her knees to her chest and laid her head on top. Her heart shattered into a million pieces over and over like it had the night officers had shown up on her doorstep to deliver the news. Her fiancé, the man she was supposed to spend the rest of her life with, had been unceremoniously ripped from her life and pronounced dead. She had a drunk driver to thank. The man had been three sheets to the wind and had passed at the wheel when he'd robbed Lily and her fiancé of their happily ever after.

Broken glass lay shattered on her tile, her wall left wet and streaked by the wine.

"You did this. It's your fault," she screamed up into the ceiling, not knowing if he'd left the premises for good or was roaming around in the other rooms.

Lily stayed in the bath until the water cooled and her tears dried. Every night and day, it was the same. She was walking around like a zombie, unable to find the joy in what she used to, unable to find taste in her favorite food. It didn't matter; nothing did.

She got out of the bath and dried off, not bothering with her hair. She slid into her bed and let the darkness take her away. Her only prayer was that she didn't dream of him. Those dreams only made her miss him more.

2 CHAPTER

Lily changed into a pair of sweats and pulled her hair back in a ponytail. She didn't bother with any makeup. What was the point? She had no one to look beautiful for, no one who would even notice.

A banging on her door sounded through the house, and she plodded down the stairs when all she really wanted to do was go back to bed.

"Hold your horses," she hollered while turning off the security system and unlocking the three locks that her dad's company had installed. She flung the door open, ready to tear into whichever relative had been sent to check on her.

"Who the hell are you?" the handsome, yet rude, stranger on her deck said.

"Excuse you, asshole, is that how you were taught to greet all strangers?" She crossed her arms over her chest. "Who the hell are you?"

"Do you kiss your momma with that mouth?"

"I could ask you the same." Lily narrowed her eyes. "You have until the count of five to get the hell off my property, or I'm calling the law."

The man's lips twisted at the corner. His gaze travelled down to her bare feet before settling on her face. "Doll, you've got that all wrong." He brushed by her, walking into the house as though he owned it. He dropped a duffel bag by her couch. "This is my house."

"In your dreams, buddy. I've got a mortgage that proves otherwise. I bought the place two weeks ago." She walked over to her phone and picked it up while keeping one eye on the stranger. She pressed a few buttons on her security panel and she was the one wearing the smirk. "You have less than five minutes to get off my property."

He nudged some of the boxes out of his way with his foot and plopped down on the couch. "Not until you tell me who the hell you are and how you got in here."

"Suit yourself." She grabbed her gun from her purse and placed it in the waistband of her pants before walking into her kitchen to start her pot of coffee. "I asked you to leave, nicely. I'm not asking again."

"I'm not going anywhere until you answer some questions."

She waited for her coffee pot to brew while leaning backward to get a better view to see if he'd headed her warning.

The jerk still had his oversized, dirty boots propped up on her coffee table and had his fingers laced behind his head. She took a sip from her warm mug while propping her shoulder against the archway.

Lily's cell phone rang and she pulled it out of her pocket.

"Uncle Butch and John are in route. Are you all right?" her dad asked practically breathless.

"Some guy showed up claiming this is his house. I asked him to leave and he won't."

"Lily, did he touch you?"

"Of course not." She tsked. "He's still living. I would have had his ass sprawled on the floor. He's a big guy, but I can take him."

The stranger watched her while she talked on the phone. His gaze traveling over her body once again, making her stomach knot and twist under his deep hypnotic eyes. *Oh, I don't think so.* She stiffened, not only fighting his presence but also her body's response. Her cheeks heated as she took a deep, calming breath. Just a few more minutes and this would be over, the jerk gone, and her house quiet again, just the way she liked it.

"I don't remember you."

She covered the speaker with her hand. "That's because you don't live here, schmuck. Are you drunk? Maybe mentally challenged or lost?"

So much for maintaining her cool.

"You're the delusional one, doll face." His lips twisted in a mocking grin. Had he baited her for a reaction?

She uncovered the speaker. "He called me doll face. Can I shoot him in the knee if I promise not to kill him? Just hurt him a little."

"Not unless you want to ruin your new floors. Lily, ETA is two minutes. Don't hurt him until they get there."

"Fine," she answered. She heard the crunch of the gravel as the tires screeched to a halt in her yard, five seconds before boots thudded against her porch. "I warned you."

Uncle Butch and John had their weapons drawn and at the ready. They stepped in and gauged the situation.

"Who's he?" John asked.

She shrugged. "He claims he owns the place."

"That's not possible," Uncle Butch announced. "Claire was with you when you signed the paperwork."

The annoying stranger rose from his spot and walked to the banister; he ran his finger over the design. "My great-great-granddaddy built this place with his bare hands. This house has been in my family for generations." He turned back to Lily. "You're the one who's trespassing. All of you."

Lily rolled her eyes. Her cousin, John, took up position beside her. "I think you're the one who needs to leave." John motioned with his gun toward the door. "Let's go."

Aunt Claire's heels clicked as she walked up onto the porch. Her perfectly styled hair and pressed shirt made her look crisp and stylish. She stopped at the open door. Her gaze went around the room, landing on the stranger. "You must be Danny Sawyer's son, Dylan. You're the spitting image of your daddy."

Lily pointed accusingly at the stranger. "You know him?"

She nodded. "That's why I'm here. I heard a rumor he was coming to town. I just didn't believe my ears until I heard that he'd shown up here."

The stranger folded his arms over his big, muscular chest in defiance, and his jaw clenched. Whoa, Nelly. Down, girl. Her physical response to the stranger was unheard of, even unwanted. Lilly took another sip of her coffee.

"Where is the old man?"

Claire frowned as she walked farther into the living room and right up to the stranger. She rested her palm on his arm. "He had a heart attack about two months ago and died. We tried to find you, but no one had a good number for you or an address. We even hired a PI to track you down, but you don't tend to leave an electronic footprint, which might I add, is very impressive. We checked with old neighbors, anything we could find." She shook her head. "I'm so sorry for your loss."

Dylan sat down on one of the stairs and rested his elbows on his knees. He cupped his head in his hand.

"If there's anything you need," Aunt Claire said and pulled out one of her cards, handing it to him. "Just call us. We're all here to help. Your father was a good man."

"Thanks," Dylan answered.

Aunt Claire walked over to Lily and hugged her. "I'm glad you're home. I'm going to take the guys with me, if that's okay. Dylan isn't a threat."

John didn't move from her side. "I think I'll stay until he leaves."

Lily ushered them all to the door. "Don't be ridiculous. He's just in shock and I, for one, know what it's like to have the rug pulled out from under you without warning. I'm sorry I bothered you guys, but I can take it from here."

John gave the guy one last look, and she did too. Dylan's head was still drooped, and he looked like a man who'd lost his best friend. "I'll call if there's any more trouble. I promise."

Her cousin, John, was eighteen years older, married with kids of his own. Growing up she'd worshiped the ground he walked on, and that hadn't changed. He was a good man, always nice and kind to her, understanding that she was special. His hesitation didn't surprise her. It rammed home the reason she'd come back to Southall. She needed her family, maybe not every five minutes checking in on her, but right now, she was exactly where she needed to be.

Lily closed the door behind them and leaned back against the wood. She walked over to the stranger and held out her hand.

He looked at her palm in question before looking up at her face.

"Come on."

His brows dipped.

She shook her hand. "Trust me."

"I don't even know you."

"Lily Bennett." She wiggled her hand again. "Now just trust me."

He gripped her hand, and she pulled him to his feet. His warm, callused palm was a foreign feel against her skin. She dropped her hold and led him into the kitchen. She set her coffee cup down on the counter and opened the fridge.

"What can I get you to drink? I don't have much, but I've got water, tea, beer, wine or whisky." She glanced over her shoulder.

"Whisky." His voice came out husky. Sadness filled his once-amused eyes.

"Whisky it is," she answered and opened a cabinet, trying to reach up to grab the bottle. She strained, berating herself that she hadn't kept it within reach. She was five feet four and resourceful. She was just about to jump up on the counter when his big body pressed in behind her.

"Let me get that for you."

His woodsy smell engulfed her. His hard body pressed up behind her. It had been six months since she'd been this close to any man other than her fiancé. She shook the thoughts away and waited for him to move so she could go to the other cabinet and get two glasses down. She dropped a couple of ice cubes in both and moved to sit at her little kitchen table.

Retaking his seat, he waited. She unscrewed the lid and poured them each a glass. She left the lid off the bottle and set it down in the middle between them.

She held up her glass. "A toast to your dad?"

"To my dad. May he rest in peace." He gave a solemn nod and clinked his glass to hers. She took a sip, letting the amber liquid burn going down her throat. He downed his in one gulp and poured another.

He took another sip and this time, drank it slower.

"I'm sorry for your loss." Lily finished her glass and walked to the sink to rinse it out. She turned the faucet on, and the knob shot up and hit the ceiling. Water sprayed up into the air like a fire hydrant with a blown top. She squealed and struggled to turn the metal piece that had been attached to the knob, but her fingers slipped, unable to get a good hold. The gushing water was soaking her from head to toe.

His large hands brushed her aside before wrestling the shaft into the off position. He turned around and held out his hands. Water dripped down from his hair over his face. His entire shirt was soaked, giving her a glimpse of his muscles beneath. They both were soaked to the core and looked like drowned rats. Dylan tossed his head back and laughed a full-belly laugh that made her smile despite their predicament.

"Do you have tools?"

She nodded and pointed to the pantry. She walked out the back door and returned with a mop and bucket. "I'm so sorry."

He chuckled from inside the pantry, calling back out to her, "It's not your fault. It's my great-great-granddaddy's."

"I'm sure the plumbing has been replaced since he built it," she answered pulling the wet fabric away from her chest. Thank god her shirt wasn't white, or they might be having an entirely different conversation, if they were speaking at all.

Dylan walked out of the pantry with her pink tool bag and lifted it in the air. His lips twitched. "Pink?"

"They work just the same." She shrugged.

He set the bag on the counter next to the sink. "I need to turn your water off. Are you okay with that?"

"You know, I could just call a plumber. You don't have to do this."

"I know this house better than any plumber. It was my relative's crappy plumbing skills that got you into this mess. I'll fix them. That's the least I can do."

Lily held the handle of the mop to her chest. Her heart ached for the man who was supposed to live long enough to endure her honey-do lists. A twinge of guilt settled in her belly. Maybe it was the bad-boy persona that Dylan gave off, or maybe it was just because he was a good looking man. Regardless, she didn't understand how easily she could be attracted to another man?

"Thanks." Her words came out a whisper. She shoved the broken promises to the back of her mind, dropped her gaze to the wet floor, and started cleaning. It was the one thing that helped her forget. She'd heard tales that her Aunt Abby was the same way. Her aunts and uncles could all judge Aunt Abby's moods by how clean her house was. Lily smiled at the thought and continued cleaning. Dylan moved around her, his mind set on fixing the faucet, hers on cleaning the floors. If her mom were to come over right now, Lily would have a one-way ticket to the loony bin. Either that or she'd be pushing Dylan to take Lily out on a date.

An hour later, they'd both changed and were sitting on her couch. She clutched a cup of coffee while he had a glass of tea. "Thanks for your help."

"You're welcome. I'm sorry about earlier." He shook his head. "I..."

She waved away his comment. "I understand." She cleared her throat. "So what are you going to do now?"

Dylan shrugged. "I've been gone overseas for the last five years, out of touch with everyone and everything. I guess you could say my specialty is security work. I'm sure I'll find a job." His eyes glazed as he stared off in the direction of the stairs. "I was going to stay with my dad."

He shook his head and set the glass down on the coffee table before standing. "I'm sorry for the intrusion. I should be on my way. I'm sure I can find a hotel for now."

Everything was already booked for the holidays. She didn't even have to call to verify. She'd grown up in the small town. She knew how busy things got during these times. She rose from her seat and chewed her bottom lip while hesitating. She warred in her mind about telling him he could stay. He was a complete stranger. Well, not a stranger to the house, but to her. He picked up his bag and was at the door before she made up her mind.

"You know what? The hotels are probably booked for holidays, and this house is plenty big. You can stay here until you figure things out. I mean, it's my fault that you don't have anywhere to go."

"You didn't kill my dad."

She wrapped her arms around her stomach. "No, I didn't, but I could use your help. If you hadn't been here when the faucet broke, I'm sure the whole house would be flooded."

"I'm sure your boyfriend with the gun would have come back to fix it."

Lily's lips twitched. "That wasn't my boyfriend. He's my cousin, and I'm sure you're right. He would have." She shrugged. "I would have just been too stubborn to ask."

Dylan gave a slow nod. His eyes strayed to her hand, and he gestured to her fingers. "Is your fiancé going to mind?"

Her heart clenched just thinking about Joe and then fell into the pit of her stomach, and she lowered her gaze. "I'm sure you're right, if he was alive." She looked up and met Dylan's dark gaze. "He died six months ago."

The awkward silence grew between them. It was the typical response she was getting used to. "I'm sorry."

"Now you understand the overprotective family." She cleared her throat. "So you're actually doing me a favor. They'll think I'm getting back to my old self, and if I'm lucky, that will give me a little breathing room." She shrugged. "And you'll have a temporary place to lay your head."

She held up her hand. "You aren't like a serial killer, are you? You're not going to chop me up in my sleep?"

He chuckled but didn't answer.

She pulled the gun from her waistband. "I have to warn you, I'm a pretty good shot and a light sleeper."

His grin grew bigger. "I bet you're just full of surprises, Lily Bennett."

"Okay, well now that's settled. Let me show you to your room, and then I'll make us some breakfast."

****

Dylan followed up the stairs behind the petite blonde. From the second he'd laid eyes on her and gotten a glimpse of her feisty attitude, he wanted to delve deeper beneath her sad eyes. His dad's death had shocked him, and what he'd told her was true. For the most part. He'd been overseas, and even though he hadn't known about his father, he'd gotten another call of sorts. One he knew would one day come. All of the males in his family, from his great-great granddaddy down to his father, had received the same beacon. The signal was the reason the house had been built to begin with. The old bastard had been waiting for his great-great grandmother's call. It came and called him home, just like Lily's cry could be felt across the sea.

Lily Bennett was a hot mess, and so was his...er...her house. He ran his hands up the banister, a habit he'd yet to break from his childhood. She glanced over her shoulder when she reached the top.

"Which one was yours?" she asked, pointing toward the open doors.

He gestured to the last one at the end of the hall. The one across from hers. Even if it hadn't been, he would have claimed it just the same. "That one on the end."

She gave a slow nod. "I bet you were a troublemaker as a kid."

He grinned and wondered if she'd be surprised to know how accurate she'd been. She didn't know his story. There was no way she could.

"What makes you say that?" he asked, curiosity getting the better of him.

"Room across from the master. I'm guessing they were afraid you were sneaking out at night. With a room so close, they probably thought they'd be able to hear you."

He chuckled but didn't respond.

She stopped just outside the door and let him walk in. "You can just move my boxes out of the way. I'll come up and get them later. The sheets and comforter are clean, and the bed is new. Feel free to use the dresser or closet or whatever you need."

He walked into the room and turned in place.

"What happened to the stuff that was in here? Do you still have it?"

She nodded. "They moved the furniture to the storage shed, and I believe they put some things up in the attic."

He met her gaze. "Just out of curiosity, why didn't you get rid of it?"

She shrugged. "That stuff isn't junk. It's attached to someone's memories, even if they aren't mine. I couldn't bring myself to get rid of any of it. Unlike Aunt Claire, I didn't know about you, but I figured the previous owners had relatives somewhere, and one day they might come looking for it."

He tilted his head. "How did you know?"

She smiled, her eyes lighting up for the first time since he had arrived. "The banister and the fireplace. I figured the guy who put that amount of detail and love into this house probably showered his family with more. Love like that is...rare."

Dylan tossed his duffel bag onto the bed and mumbled under his breath, "You have no idea."

3 CHAPTER

Lily jogged back down the stairs. She was an idiot. She didn't take strangers in off the streets. Granted, he wasn't a complete stranger to all of the Bennetts, but she didn't know anything about him other than his rock-hard abs beneath the wet shirt, his strong hands that turned off the water, or his sexy-ass grin. It was official; he needed to go.

She pulled out a carton of eggs and grabbed the pancake batter and bacon from the fridge. Dylan was a big guy, probably with a big appetite. She fired off a text to her mother, letting her know what was going on and telling her not to worry, as if that was possible.

She mentioned that she'd bring him by the café and introduce them once he got settled in. Lily tossed the phone onto the counter and started making breakfast. The smell of bacon frying made her stomach growl. She couldn't remember the last time she'd eaten or why she was hungry now. She just was.

Out of the corner of her eye, she found Dylan leaning against the doorframe of the entryway. He was watching her cook.

"You're just in time."

"It smells great," he announced and pushed off the wall, walking into the kitchen. He moved to stand beside her, and his arm brushed hers, sending the butterflies in her belly into a tizzy. Seriously?

"Do you need any help?"

"Nope, have a seat." She placed the plates of food on the table. "I can't promise the food will be good, but I can guarantee it won't kill you."

"Bonus." He grinned in that way she was becoming used to. It was sly and inviting and mysterious all at the same time. Behind those eyes, and in his mind, he was probably saying...'sucker' and scheming ways to get his house back. Dylan winked. Was the timing coincidence, or was that his way of saying she'd hit the nail on the head? The timing of his teasing gesture was impeccable. Was she dealing with a mind reader along with a psycho who was going to chop her up in her sleep? *You're losing it.* In her mind, she'd be dead by midnight, but in reality....probably not at all. She rolled her eyes, fighting the urge to grin at her silly banter. Thank god he couldn't hear her thoughts.

Dylan made them both a cup of coffee and placed them on the table.

"Thanks," she said and picked up her coffee.

"It's the least I could do." He picked up a piece of bacon and took a bite. "I'll return the favor and cook you dinner." He grinned. "I can't promise how it will taste." He grinned. "But it won't kill you."

"Bonus," she echoed.

The air around her felt lighter than previous mornings. Maybe it was the company or just her new home. Whatever it was, she'd take the momentary reprieve as a breath of fresh air. He was like a new puzzle to solve and the thought of getting out of her head and back into the land of the living, seemed more inviting by the minute.

"I'm going into town today. Would you like to come with me?"

He took another bite of his bacon. She could see the wheels turning. "I think I'll stay."

Lily tsked while palming her coffee mug. "Let me rephrase." She grinned. "My mom wants to make sure you aren't a serial killer, so we can either go to her café, where we can leave when we're ready, or she's coming here, and when I say she'll come here, I mean she'll bring the entire family and we may never get rid of them." Lily gave a slight shake of her head and a pretend shiver. "Trust me, you don't want that."

"Sounds like I'm going to town." An easy smile played at the corners of his mouth. "I need to talk to my dad's attorney anyway and see what else may need to be taken care of."

****

Dylan entered the café behind Lily. A man and woman wearing name tags hugged her in passing on their way back to the counter. The front windows were decorated in snowmen made with spray paint. Christmas lights were strung around the walls and windows throughout the café; the workers wore Santa hats on their heads, and a bell, complete with mistletoe, was above the door. "She goes all out for Christmas."

Lily made her way around the counter and started making them both drinks. "It's her favorite time of the year."

Dylan rested his elbows on the counter. "Yet I don't remember seeing even one decoration up at your house."

Lily released a deep sigh. "I'm avoiding it this year." She handed him one of the coffee's she'd just poured.

"Not in the Christmas spirit?"

"Would you be if you'd lost your fiancé and had gone running home?"

"Touché," he answered and followed her to one of the booths, sliding in across from her. He took his time to take in the coffee shop.

"Mom's probably in the office." She grinned and waved her fingers in hello to one of the security cameras.

"Your family sure believes in security."

"Five, four, three, two..." Lily didn't even get to one before her mother strolled out of the back room and headed straight for them.

"Well, there you are." Her mom smiled brightly as she squeezed into the booth next to Lily. "You must be Dylan."

"I forgot how fast word travels in this town," Dylan replied, watching a spark of amusement shine in Lily's eyes.

Lily leaned forward. "It's a gift, but now...Aunt Claire gives everyone a run for their money. She has her finger on the pulse of the town."

Lily's mom watched the exchange with a trained eye. He could tell that she had been assessing him from earlier, even before she sat down. Maybe as soon as they'd walked in the door. The woman held out her hand. "Emma Bennett."

"Dylan Sawyer, it's nice to meet you." He shook her hand.

"Danny's kid. Your dad was a good man. I'm sorry for your loss."

"Thanks," Dylan answered before taking a sip of his coffee.

"I hear you're staying with my daughter." Emma pegged him with a look his own mother would have been proud of. "There's nothing I need to worry about, right?" Her words weren't a question, more like a silent threat.

He bit back his smile, knowing if he showed the tiniest hint of amusement that Emma Bennett would drag him out of the café by the ear. Clearing his throat, he answered, "No, ma'am. I'll protect her with my life."

"With your life? That's interesting." Emma leaned back, her head tilted to the side. "Who's going to protect her from you?"

Dylan's lips twitched. "She's already threatened to kick my butt and shoot me. She must get that from you."

The tension in Emma's shoulders eased, and she replaced her suspicion with a smile. "Me and her father, or maybe it's her cousin John, Uncle Butch, or even Uncle Mike. He's a cop, you know."

Dylan chuckled. "I didn't, but I'll keep that in mind."

"See that you do." She turned her gaze to Lily. "Christopher was in here this morning asking about you."

Lily closed her eyes. "Tell me you didn't."

When her mother didn't answer, Lily's eyes popped open. "Mom...tell me you didn't."

She shrugged. "You need to get back in the game. You and Christopher used to be close. I think you need someone like him right now, even if it's just as a good friend." She grinned and slid from the booth.

"I'm not looking for any more friends." Lily's brows dipped.

"Well, If something more comes out of it, then that would be great too."

"Mother..."

She shrugged. "I worry. I don't want you to grow up to be an old bitter cat lady. You need love. You're young and beautiful, and I just want you to be happy."

Lily dropped her gaze to the Styrofoam coffee cup in her hands. She dug her nails into the side, carving her name as she answered. "Six months is not enough time." She raised her gaze to meet her mom's. "Not everyone can have a relationship like you and Daddy. I had my chance, and I lost it."

Dylan could read the worry in Emma's eyes. A conversation that maybe they'd had before. She was worried and rightly so, if Lily had given up. He'd known her a little over two hours and already knew she was pretending to be okay when she was anything but okay.

"Sweetie, you can't stop living because you lost him. Celebrate the time you had with him. He'd want you to be happy."

"I know, Mom; trust me."

Lily slid from the booth and raised her brows at Dylan, prodding him to get up. "We have to run some errands." She kissed her mother's cheek. "I'll call you later."

"It was nice meeting you, Mrs. Bennett."

"You too, Dylan."

Dylan followed Lily out of the café. He'd witnessed their exchange. Did he agree with Lily? No. She was due for a love like none she'd ever experienced, not even with her fiancé. She was due to experience that passion and desire and everything in between, only it was going to be with him, not some ass named Christopher. Even the mention of another man, with sights set on Lily, aggravated him, and he hadn't even met the guy.

"You know she's right." Dylan slowed his step to walk beside her. "You will find it again when you least expect it."

"Please." She glanced up at him. "Not you too."

He held up his hands in surrender. "You're right. None of my business." He pointed to his father's attorney's office across the street. "I'm going to run in and talk to Mr. Stanford. I'll meet you back at the house?"

"Sure," she answered, slowing her step. "Don't you need me to wait and give you a ride?"

He shook his head, playing his cards close to his chest. The less she knew right now, the better. "I'll manage."

Dylan walked her to the car and held the door open for her to get in. "Be careful."

She arched her brow. "You too."

He closed her door and watched her drive down Main Street before he crossed the road to the attorney's office.

The bell above the door rang as he entered the law office. Sylvia, the receptionist, glanced up from her magazine. Her eyes widened. "Mr. Sawyer."

"Is he in?" Dylan questioned while pointing toward the closed door.

Sylvia quickly rose to her feet. She knew what he was about to do. Cute, she thought she could stop him. "Is he expecting you?"

Dylan gave her a terse nod and moved with purposeful strides into the attorney's office unannounced.

Franklin was standing at the filing cabinet when Dylan burst in.

"You sold my house!" Dylan growled.

"We couldn't reach you. You left us no choice."

Dylan stormed over to the attorney and grabbed him by the lapels of his suit. "I bet you didn't even try."

"I sent you certified mail and have the receipt that you got it."

Dylan ground his teeth. "I never got anything."

Franklin's tone was apologetic. "Your dad owed back taxes for the last two years. I. Had. No. Choice. When we couldn't reach you and you never inquired about the documents..."

Dylan released the attorney and plopped down in one of the leather chairs. His day was just getting better by the minute. First the girl and now the house. He let out a lengthy sigh.

Fixing the lapels of his suit, Franklin closed the door and rounded his desk. "I know this is a shock, but it's true. Your dad had debt. The money in his account wasn't enough to cover the taxes. I'm sorry."

"I sent my dad over a thousand a month. What was he using it for?"

Franklin pulled out a file from his desk and flipped it open. He thumbed through the documents and pulled out a piece of paper from the stack. He leaned over the desk and handed it to Dylan.

The document was a bank statement. The largest of the transactions were for construction equipment and the hardware store.

"What the hell was he doing?" Dylan asked. His gaze went to the top of the form to verify it was his father's.

"He was looking for the Heart."

Dylan lifted his gaze to meet Franklin's and tossed the bank statement across the desk. "It's a myth. The ruby doesn't exist."

"He came into my office about two weeks before he died. He was excited and kept pacing back and forth. He said he'd found a map, and he knew where to find the Heart. He was mumbling. I thought he'd finally lost his mind."

Dylan collapsed back in his chair. He'd grown up hearing stories about pirates hiding their bounty on his family's property. Rumor had it that his great-great-grandfather had made a deal with the thief but died before divulging the location. It was a myth, nothing more. Wasn't it?

"He didn't tell you where?"

Franklin placed the document back in the folder. "Not even a hint." He pulled out another form and handed it to Dylan.

The certification held a signature all right, but it wasn't Dylan's. "That's not my signature. Where did you have this delivered?"

"Your last apartment in Virginia."

Dylan shook his head in frustration. "I haven't been state-side in five years, and I can prove it."

"Hmm." Franklin eased back in his chair, resting his elbows on the arms. He steepled his fingers in thought. "I might be able to work that angle. Let me look into the signature."

Dylan dropped his foot and sat forward in his chair. "Let me know what you find out before you proceed with anything."

"What if the Heart is on the property?"

Dylan rose, wrote down his cell phone number, and handed it to the attorney. "It's a myth."

"But..."

Dylan straightened his shoulders. "No buts....I'm staying out at the property with Lily Bennett and plan to go through my dad's things. We've had several generations of families on that property. Don't you think if it was real that we'd have found it before now?"

Franklin gave a slow nod. "I'll see what I can do about the house."

"Thanks." Dylan walked out of the office without a backward glance. What the hell had his dad been doing, and what clue had he found?

4 CHAPTER

Dylan made his way down Main Street. The idea of the Heart being a real possibility was firmly planted in his mind. Was it really possible that, after all these years, he'd found a clue, a map no less? Dylan's mind replayed the last time they'd spoken. There had been a rising excitement in his voice.

Dylan walked aimlessly, on autopilot, on a path he'd travelled many times before. He stopped across the street, staring over at Rosa's Italian Restaurant. His gaze travelled up the railing to the balcony on the second floor. Potted plants, holding colorful blooms, sat outside. The curtains were open, but the apartment was dark. Dylan jogged across the street and walked in.

"As I live and breathe," Rosa Sanchez called from behind the counter.

"Rosa." Dylan grinned at her familiar face. No matter how long he stayed away, some things stayed the same. He crossed the room, pulling the old woman into a hug. "It's been a long time."

"Too long, young man."

Dylan let her go and tossed his arm around her shoulder. "How's business?"

"Business is good, but you would already know that if you ever read the financials I sent you."

"I moved. No forwarding address." Dylan grinned and walked into the kitchen, grabbing a freshly baked breadstick from a batch still cooling on the rack. He inhaled a deep breath, taking in all of the herbal essences that filled the air. He spotted a pot of sauce, raised the lid, grabbed a plastic spoon, and tasted the concoction. He grinned. "You're still making my recipe from scratch."

She gave him a motherly smile. "It's one of my best sellers." She shrugged and stirred the white sauce with a ladle. "By the way, in case you don't check your bank account either, you're a millionaire now."

"Well, you're the best partner a guy could have." Dylan kissed her cheek before taking a bite of the breadstick. "If it wasn't for you, letting me play in your kitchen when I was younger, I never would have concocted that recipe. If you hadn't believed in me, it wouldn't even be on the market."

"You give me too much credit." Rosa's cheeks flushed a hint of pink.

"I don't give you enough." Dylan walked over to the fridge and pulled out a water bottle, debating whether to make himself a plate of food. The smells were calling to him, begging him and tempting him to try some of the food he'd craved since the day he'd left. "I sure did miss you."

"I'm sorry about your father."

Dylan's appetite diminished. "Me too. I wish I would have been here."

Rosa rubbed Dylan's back, the way a mother might when trying to console her child. "It was unexpected. You couldn't have known."

Dylan gestured toward the back door. "Anyone upstairs in my apartment?"

She shook her head. "I've kept it for you just the way you left it. I try and keep it clean and ready. I figured you might return when you found out about your dad."

She walked over to the wall near the door and grabbed a set of keys hanging on the hook. She handed them to him. "The apartment is ready for you, and your motorcycle had a tune-up about a month ago. It's still in storage, but the mechanic comes by periodically to make sure it's running perfectly."

Dylan pulled her into his arms and kissed the top of her head. "You're the best boss ever."

She chuckled. "I'm not your boss anymore. I'm your partner."

"Partners in crime." He winked. "I'm staying out at dad's house, but I'll be in from time to time."

"You better. I'll keep your table ready," she called out after him as he headed toward the back door.

He lifted his water bottle up in acknowledgement before walking out. He took the stairs two at a time to the second-floor landing.

He unlocked the door and stepped into his private sanctuary, his home away from home. The scent of the Italian herbs from the kitchen below travelled through the vents, filling the space with the fresh aroma. Sunlight from the open blinds lit the small space, his one-bedroom, one-bath hideaway that he kept in town for emergencies or just for those times he wanted to be alone, free to be himself. Not many people in town knew he had his own place. He'd always stayed with his dad when he was home. This place was his secret. If Lily Bennett believed he had somewhere else to go, she wouldn't have agreed to let him stay, and then it might make it more difficult to get her to trust him. That would ruin his plans.

He needed all the help he could get. His heart fluttered with renewed hope that the call had finally come. Even if she didn't realize what she'd done, she'd called him home. He was here; she was here, and their lives were just beginning. The search for the Heart was just beginning. His life was changing at a rate that made it hard to keep up.

Dylan tossed the keys onto the kitchen bar. He flipped on the light, out of habit, to get a better view of the place. He gazed around the familiar room. The place was just as he'd left it. Although what was once new was a bit older, it was still home. He walked through the living room and into his bedroom, familiarizing himself with what he'd left behind. His tan comforter was clean and pressed, and the bed was made. He glanced into the closet. Some of his clothes were still hanging inside. His specially-made backpack that concealed his riffle sat on the closet floor. He grabbed it and slung it over his shoulder. He walked into the fully stocked bathroom. The porcelain sparkled, with no dust in sight. Rosa Sanchez was a savior and a saint. It was true that Dylan had made them both rich, but Rosa had given him something much more. She'd given him her faith when not many would. Lily had guessed he was a bad boy, but the extent of his shenanigans remained hidden in his sealed juvenile records. He wasn't a saint.

Rosa had given him his first job, his first taste of independence, and her trust, when not many people in town would. She treated him like her own child and never gave up on the type of man he could be, molding him into a better version of himself. He owed this woman his soul.

He walked back into the living room, grabbed his keys off the breakfast bar, and locked up the place as he left.

****

Lily walked in her front door and paused. In the corner of the room, the ghost of an old man was rocking in a rocker she'd yet to take to the attic. He watched her with an eagle eye as she studied him.

"You can see me?" he asked in a gravelly voice that spoke volumes of his years of smoking.

"You must be related to Dylan," she countered and walked farther into the room, dropping her purse on the table.

"Dylan's my great-grandson. I'm Walter Sawyer." He grinned.

She sat down in the recliner and clasped her fingers in her lap. "I'm Lily, and it's a pleasure to meet you. I hope you aren't one of those ghosts that get territorial because I really love this place."

"I hear you cry at night."

Lily frowned, her heart aching at the thought. "I tend to do that when I'm sad."

"You won't be when your friend leaves."

"My friend?"

"Joe." The apparition stopped rocking."

"I know," she answered. Her heart ached at his name. Her voice sounded like a whisper in the room.

"Dylan will make you happy."

She gave Walt a small smile. The ghost was like her mother, each trying to push her into moving on, something she wasn't ready to do. "I think he's a little mad that I live in his house."

"Your house," Walt corrected. "Your soul knows this place is home. Your soul recognizes him."

The house, yes, but him? She felt chemistry, but that didn't equal anything other than a potential fling. Nothing significant, nothing that justified handing over her heart....again. No, not him, just the house.

Her front door opened, and she glanced over her shoulder to make sure it was Dylan. He came in carrying a couple of grocery bags. His brows dipped as he first looked at her and then in the direction of the chair.

"Can you see him?" she asked, knowing that the question might give her abilities away.

"See who?"

"Never mind." Well, that answered her question. Maybe he'd just seen the chair move.

He walked through the living room, lifting up the grocery bags. "I hope steaks are all right for dinner."

"Steaks sound great." She rose from her chair and followed behind Dylan. She gave Walt one more glance as he fizzled out of sight.

She watched, slightly intrigued, as Dylan unwrapped the steaks, getting them ready for marinade. "How did you get back?"

"My bike," he answered

Of course he drove a bike, like Joe. And his probably wasn't a ten-speed either. She gave a slow nod. "And the car outside?"

"It's a rental I drove into town until I was sure my bike had been serviced," he answered while putting the steaks into the fridge. He rested his hip on the counter. "Why are you looking at me like that?"

A knock on the door paused her answer. "Excuse me."

He gave a slight dismissing nod and grabbed the wine out of the bag as she went to see who had shown up. Which relative was it going to be this time? If she was lucky, it was just John coming to check in on her. He was easy to appease and even easier to get rid of.

She pulled the door open. Christopher Henkel stood on her porch.

"Hi, Christopher." She tried for a smile but probably failed miserably.

"It's good to see you, Lily. So I guess it's true. You're back in town for good."

She pressed her lips together and gave a slow nod. "Yep, it true. Guess Mom told you, huh?"

He glanced over her head, looking passed her into the house and who may be inside. "Yeah, you could say that. She mentioned you wanted to go out with me."

Lily's mouth parted, as she was unable to check the shock from showing.

"Lily, honey. Who's at the door?" Dylan asked, walking up behind her. He wrapped his arms around her waist and pulled her back against his chest.

Lily momentarily stiffened in his arms. "Dylan, this is my friend Christopher."

Christopher's gaze met Dylan's before settling back on her face.

"I guess your mom was wrong."

"I'm sorry, Chris. She meant well, but I guess you can say that things with Dylan"— she glanced up at her impromptu boyfriend—"have just progressed."

Christopher took a tentative step backward. "Well...I won't keep you two."

"Thanks for stopping by," Dylan replied as they both watched Christopher leave.

Lily closed the door and spun around to face Dylan. His hands dropped to his sides, and he took an unconscious step back. "Why did you do that?"

"Your reaction at the café when your mom told you what she'd done."

Lily rested her hands on her hips and drooped her head. She met his gaze and tried to hide the irritation from her face. "Do you know what you've just done?"

"I scared away a guy who wants to date you?"

She shook her head, a smirk in place of a smile. "You've just proclaimed to all of Southall that we're dating." She could feel the headache forming behind her eyes and hear all of the questions that would soon follow. "Including my family. The only problem with that is....they aren't stupid. They'll know the truth."

He remained quiet. Was he letting the consequences of his actions sink in? Was he now worried that he'd just screwed his own reputation on top of hers?

"What's wrong with us dating for real? Am I not your type?"

She threw her hands up in the air. "Of course you are, but I'm not dating you. I'm not dating anyone. I'm not ready for that."

"Life doesn't stop because you lose someone you love. It sucks; it hurts; and there will be days when you feel like giving up, but guess what...you won't because you're too strong for that. More days are going to pass, and you've got two options.

You can let your hurt suck the life out of you, which by my guess is what is currently happening, or you can stand up and take part. I may not be an expert, but I haven't pegged you for a quitter."

She slapped him, her palm making contact with his face and leaving a red imprint of her hand. "How dare you! You don't know me. You don't know what I've been through."

He leaned into her, pinning her against the door. His eyes caressed her face, and his hands pressed against the door near her head. "You're wrong. I do know you. You're the woman who owns my house; you're the woman who met her mother head-on instead of waiting for her to come to you; you're the woman who didn't throw away my past because you knew someone, someday, would come looking for it, and you're the woman who took me in when I didn't have anywhere else to go. So yes, Lily, I may not have known you for years, but I do know you."

Her eyes searched his. Her chest heaved as desire pooled in her belly, and the want she thought she'd never feel again came back like a rush of water. Passion exploded inside of her at his words, more passion than she'd ever experienced in her life. She felt alive, and more than that, he was right.

Her arms went around his neck, and she pulled his mouth down to meet hers, crushing their lips together. He came willingly, settling his hands on her waist.

She opened her mouth in invitation, the electricity between them heightening her urgency.

He pulled her closer, and his hands caressed her sides. He kissed her back with the same passion his words had provoked. Her tongue delved into his mouth, tasting him for the first time, feeling alive for the first time in months. She needed this; she needed him.

His fingers slipped beneath the hem of her shirt, his palm cupping her breast, and she moaned into his mouth.

When he broke the kiss, the rapid beat of his heart matched hers. He slid his fingers out from beneath her shirt and rested his forehead against hers. "I'm sorry. I stepped over the line. I had no right to say those things to you."

He stepped back and she missed the heat of his body. His words penetrated through her lust-filled fog. What had she just done? Her hand covered her mouth, and she jogged up the stairs two at a time, leaving him standing in the foyer. She was already anticipating the fallout from his actions, and she'd just made it worse. She walked into her room and plopped down on her bed, falling backward. How was she going to fix this?

5 CHAPTER

Dylan dropped his head forward on his shoulders. He was an idiot. She'd run like a scared kitten, and it was all his fault. She'd said she wasn't ready, but did he believe her? No. He was thinking with the wrong part of his body. She wasn't ready for him, not yet. He'd thought he'd been doing her a favor helping her handle Chris, when in reality, the real reason was his own selfishness. Dylan had just found her. He wasn't ready to share her, not yet. He needed more time to make her see it was the two of them who belonged together.

He exhaled a deep breath, calming his body and his mind. He was going to be lucky if she didn't kick him to the curb. He'd screwed up and probably lost her before he ever even really had her. They weren't anywhere close to being on the same playing field, and his little move had just cost him the headway that he'd already made.

Dylan walked into the kitchen and grabbed a beer from the bag. He popped the top and took a long pull. This called for drastic measures, an apology that she wouldn't soon forget. This called for dessert, not just any dessert, but his infamous Italian chocolate crème cake. Dylan pulled out his phone and called Rosa at the restaurant, letting her know exactly what he needed. Not just any cake but his recipe. She promised the delivery boy would deliver it within the hour.

After putting away the groceries and putting the bottle of wine in the fridge to chill, he went about working in the kitchen, losing himself where he loved most. He turned on her radio, letting the music soothe his mind and his soul. He rolled up his sleeves and went about preparing the best meal he could. He chopped veggies for a salad, whipped up his own dressing, made a big dish of pasta with his famous sauce, seasoned the shrimp and marinated the steaks for the grill. He was bound to find something she liked, even if she didn't eat anything other than the cake. He'd find a way into her taste buds, even if he'd meant to find a way into her heart. Dylan kept busy getting things started and cooking. His stomach growled at the wonderful smells as he worked on the food in front of him.

He went to grab something from the fridge and turned to find Lily standing beneath the archway with the cake box in her hand. "How long have you been standing there?"

"I answered the door, and a kid handed me this. I assume it's yours."

"Ours." He walked over to her and pressed a kiss to her cheek. "It's my apology."

She followed him into the kitchen, lifting lids and peeking inside the dishes. "You've been busy."

"I promised you dinner," he answered while going to the fridge and pulling out the wine. He poured her a glass and handed it to her. "Dinner will be done as soon as I get the steaks off the grill. Why don't you have a seat and relax?"

Lily followed him out onto the deck and sat in one of the pool chairs. He could feel her eyes on him without even looking. He flipped the steaks.

"You went all out."

"I promised you dinner." He glanced at her before using the tongs to put the steaks on the plate. Dylan walked into the kitchen and set the steaks on the table before returning to where she was resting, looking up at the stars. He held out his hand. "Just consider it my apology for earlier."

She took his hand, and he pulled her up. "Just so we're clear, what are you apologizing for?"

She followed him into the kitchen where he worked on putting the plates together and getting everything ready for the table. "I've given it some thought, and you're right. I shouldn't have interfered with Christopher, but I couldn't help myself."

Dylan placed the salad bowl in the middle of the table.

"Why couldn't you help yourself?"

He pulled out her chair and waited for her to sit. He leaned down next to her ear. "I'm attracted to you." His words came out a whisper in her ear. "I am sorry for getting the way, but I'm not sorry for the kiss."

He placed his palms on her shoulders and ran them down her arms. "Let's eat."

He moved to sit across from her, dishing them both some salad and drizzling the dressing over the top.

Lily rested her elbows on the table and laced her fingers together, ignoring the food in front of her. She cleared her throat. "I need you to understand something."

Dylan met her steely gaze and ignored his own food. "What's that?"

She used her finger, gesturing between them both. "This, us, isn't happening."

Dylan bit back his retort, his lips tilted up in a smile. "Not yet."

She shook her head. "No....not at all."

Dylan placed his elbows on the table and clasped his fingers together. "Why not?"

"Look...I'm flattered that you find me attractive, but I love Joe, and I'll always love Joe. He was it for me."

Dylan gave a slow nod. He could tell by the determination in her eyes that she actually believed what she was saying, but he knew she'd come to a different conclusion. It might be hard for someone as strong-headed as her to realize and give in to the idea, but she'd eventually see things his way. Time was on his side. "Tell me you didn't feel the passion in our kiss or enjoy when I touched you."

"That isn't love, Dylan. That's lust, and it's a chemical reaction I can control, even if you can't."

"Lust?" He nodded, picked up his fork, and took a bite of his favorite pasta with the sauce that he'd come to love so much. "Lust is like this pasta sauce. It wets your appetite and opens you up to pleasure, but love is like knowing the recipe. Something that will last forever. Lust may very well be a chemical reaction, the invisible pull we have, but you shouldn't discard the idea of loving again. Love comes from within your heart, a feeling that consumes every fiber of your being. Don't you one day want to have that again, even if it isn't with me?"

"No." She picked up her fork and twirled some noodles around the tines before glancing over his head to something or someone behind him. He could feel the cold energy around them; the fine hairs on his arms hid the goose bumps. He wasn't a rocket scientist, but he knew when there was a ghost or two around. He steeled his desire to glance over his shoulder to find out which ghost was behind him. She returned her gaze to his. "Not if there's a chance I'll lose it."

"Nothing is a guarantee. Some might call it a leap of faith."

"Well, there you go. Faith is something I lost the day that Joe was taken from me."

"Oh, Lily, no. I never wanted that for you," an unfamiliar voice answered from behind Dylan.

Dylan remained quiet, letting the two have their moment. If Dylan couldn't talk some sense into her, maybe her dead fiancé could. He was at a loss for words. There was nothing he could say to get her to change her mind. The hurt was written in her sad eyes, the fine lines around her mouth. She wasn't ready to test the waters, even if he knew the temperature.

He lifted his glass of wine and she lifted hers. "To new friends."

She clinked his glass. "To new friends."

They both sipped. "So I guess you don't need me to be your pretend boyfriend."

She smiled, and the mood instantly lightened. "No, just my house guest."

"And handyman."

"And there is that." She put her glass down and continued eating.

They engaged in small talk about growing up in the town and their families. He steered clear of any relationship talk and gave her the night, just to feel normal and breathe in the enjoyment of each other's company. The temperature in the room warmed back to normal, the ghost that had spoken disappearing as quickly as he'd shown up. Dylan had never meant to cause her an ounce of heartache, and yet, talking about her dead fiancé had done the trick.

She wasn't ready; it was obvious, and he wasn't going to push her....yet.

They finished eating, and he went to work on the dishes while she put the leftovers away.

"Have you ever heard of the Heart?" he asked.

"The one in our chests?" she asked while putting the Tupperware away.

"No, the legend."

She gave a slow nod. "The ruby in the shape of a heart?"

"Yeah, that one."

"I heard the tale when I was a little girl. A pirate supposedly buried it along with his most prized possessions somewhere in town. It's a myth."

Dylan gave a slight shrug. "What if I told you it wasn't?"

She took a sip of her wine, and a smile lifted her lips. "You're joking, right?"

After wiping his hands on a towel, he tossed it over his shoulder, took her by the hand, and led her out the French doors to the back patio. He gestured to one of the lounge chairs and sat down on the one next to her. "There is a story of love and loss and treasure that goes along with my....your property."

Lily took a sip of her wine. "I love a good story."

"A pirate boat capsized in the rocks off the coastline. And legend has it that only the captain survived. He stumbled into town like a drowned rat without a penny to his name and only an old box clutched in his arms. My three times great-grandfather, Henry, befriended him and took him in when he had nowhere else to go. He'd often go to the shore and sit for hours at sunset and watch the waves come in, and one day Henry followed him. The way he told it, the pirate was lonely. He ached for what the water had taken from him, and every night before he drank himself to sleep, the pirate would tell Henry a tale of his travels and what he'd experienced."

"That's sad."

"The man lived a carefree life, taking what he wanted. He never answered to anyone at all until he happened upon some small town. He'd turned ill. I believe Henry explained it as a fever. He was dazed with a temperature and didn't have enough energy to even make it back to his ship. He collapsed on their beach. When he woke up, he swore he saw an angel, her hair the color of spun gold. She nursed him back to health. Her smile gave him light, and he knew instantly that he had to have her. The heavens had made her just for him and him alone."

"Did she leave with him?"

"No." Dylan took a sip of his wine. "In fact, she begged him to stay. Her parents were sick and needed her."

"Did he stay?"

Dylan shook his head. His smile dipped into a frown. "He left her and went on to live a life of misery."

Lily's lips parted before she snapped them closed. "Then he deserved what he got."

Dylan shrugged and took another sip of his wine. "Realizing his mistake, he was going to go back to her, but knew he would have to grovel, so he made a plan. He was going to find something as beautiful as she was and offer it to her and her family. Sort of as an apology."

"Huh." Lily snorted. "She didn't fall for that, did she?"

"He sailed the oceans far and wide in search of his treasure, and that was when he stole the ruby in the shape of a heart. The stone was reported to be so precious that it held mystical powers, and the owner would always hear the call of their true love."

"The same stone said to be hidden in our town?"

"One and the same," Dylan answered and swung his legs over to sit facing Lily. "The pirate became ill, and Henry took care of him, only this time he wouldn't win against his fate. He knew the illness would take his life. He placed the ruby Heart in Henry's hands, and with the last of his strength, clutched Henry's closed hands. Henry said that his breath was weak as he spoke."

"What did he say?"

"He said he'd heard her voice every night since he'd found the Heart. He heard his angel. He gave it to Henry and told him to keep it safe and said that Henry would hear his angel's call."

"And did he? Did Henry hear the call of his true love?"

Dylan nodded. "Indeed."

He couldn't tell her that, since it was still on the property, it continued to work for all of Henry's descendants. She'd think he'd lost his mind. He told her what she needed to know, and that was enough for now.

"Remarkable." Her words came out as a breath. "Where's the Heart now?"

Dylan shrugged. "I'm not sure. Years and years ago, it was reduced to a myth, although treasure hunters have come looking for it. We've never found it."

"Henry hid it?"

Dylan nodded. "That's what I've been told."

"So do you think it's in the house?"

Dylan shook his head. "I don't think so. Henry's son, Walter, built this house; so if it is, that means my great-grandfather found it."

"Then where is it?

"No one knows. Even my dad took up the hunt for the stone and thought he was getting close to finding it, but he never mentioned where he thought it might be before he died. So it remains a mystery."

"Sounds like a mystery that needs to be solved."

Dylan tried to bite back his reaction to her interest. "Are you saying you want to help me look for it?"

"Treasure hunting?" She bit her lip, her eyes sparkled with interest. "That sounds like exactly what I need. A good puzzle to figure out."

"Great." Dylan stood. "Then you better get a good night's sleep. We'll start tomorrow by going through my dad's stuff. Maybe he left us a map."

"We can only hope."

Dylan placed his palm on Lily's shoulder in passing. "Goodnight, Lily."

She looked up, her eyes glassy from the wine. "Goodnight, Dylan."

6 CHAPTER

Lily lay beneath her thick comforter, her eyes on the ceiling above, cutting every few minutes to her bedroom door where Dylan's room was across the hall. He wouldn't hurt her; she knew it in her soul, but that didn't explain the rapid beating of her heart. That single kiss had left her breathless; the touch of his hand on her skin had awakened her. Her body and need had betrayed her, and she'd acted on pure desire. A chemical reaction she wouldn't succumb to again. She pushed those thoughts out of her head and concentrated on their other conversation. She replayed the bit about the pirate in her head.

"If he heard her voice, then it was true love, and the jerk left her," Lily mumbled to herself, mad that the pirate had caused his angel to be unhappy, and for what....a life of misery. "Figures. It's probably crap. Just a story made up by some delusional guy on his death bed. Leaving behind enough detail and intrigue to be passed down to keep generations looking for a treasure that doesn't exist."

"Lily." Joe's voice sounded throughout her room.

She closed her eyes, not wanting to see the same disappointing look that he'd given her in the kitchen when she and Dylan had been talking about love and lust.

"Go away, Joe. I'm tired."

She stayed that way, unable to face him, unable to reconcile the kiss she'd just been thinking about and the man who was supposed to be her last first kiss, unsure if he'd left. She let her exhaustion sink in and pull her into a deep sleep.

Lily's eyes shot open, unsure what had woken her. She glanced around the master suite in a daze. Her racing heart slowed when she saw that nothing was out of place. She heard the soft giggles of a little girl.

"I can hear you," Lily mumbled while pushing herself to sit up. "You can come out now."

The little girl ghost walked out of Lily's closet. "You talk in your sleep."

"Be glad I don't sing."

"You're funny."

"I've been called worse. Who are you?"

The little girl grinned and stepped closer. "I'm Mel."

Lily nodded and rose from the bed. "Well, Mel..." She glanced over to the little girl standing near the bed. "I live here now too, so we're going to have to set some ground rules."

Mel pushed out her bottom lip. "I don't like rules."

Lily shrugged her shoulders. "Sorry, but you can't play in my room when I'm here."

"But...."

"No buts. My room is off-limits. Feel free to haunt the rest of the house if you'd like, but not here. Now if you'll excuse me, I have to take a shower and get ready to go find treasure." Lily began pulling clothes out of her drawers.

The little girl's eyes opened wide. "Treasure? You mean the Heart, don't you?"

Lily eased the dresser closed and turned to face the little girl. Her blonde hair was up in pigtails and she wore overalls with a flowered shirt. "What do you know about it? Is it real?"

"Duh." The little girl grinned. "Of course it's real. If you were playing Marco Polo, I would have told you the other day that you weren't just hot but burning up." Mel covered her mouth and giggled again.

Well, that didn't help. She'd already been all through the house and toured the property. It could have been anywhere. Lily clutched her clothes tightly to her chest. "Is it in the house or on the property?"

The little girl giggled and skipped back into the closet. Lily followed and watched her disappear out of sight.

Lily went about taking a shower and getting ready for the day while pondering the idea that she might have missed seeing a big ruby somewhere on the property. Something like that would have stuck out. She would have zoned in on it, wouldn't have she? The little girl had to be teasing. There was no other explanation. Lily trotted down the stairs and into the kitchen to find Dylan walking in carrying wood. His face was clean-shaven, sweat beaded on his brow, and he was wearing a red flannel shirt over a T-shirt.

His muscles bunched as he held the wood clutched in his arms. Lumberjack wasn't her type, but damn if Dylan wasn't. He made her ache and want things that she'd already resigned herself to never having again. It was as though he'd awakened a sex-crazed, hungry beast that had been dormant for way too long. What kind of woman did that make her, having thoughts about another man? One who wasn't her dead fiancé?

"You didn't have to do that. I could have bought some precut stuff from town and had it delivered."

He tsked and shouldered past her. "Why would you do that when you have a handyman at your disposal?"

Lily bit her lip and watched as he set the wood near the fireplace. She hesitated asking him about the little girl. If she were to mention the name or say that she'd talked to a ghost, it was possible that Dylan might think she was a bit crazy. She decided against it, keeping what Mel had told her as her little secret and making a mental note to ask her more questions when she saw her again.

Dylan got a water bottle from the fridge and took a long gulp before pulling out a casserole dish. He handed it to her. "It's ready to go, just put it in the oven on 350 for thirty minutes and breakfast will be ready."

Lily turned on the oven and waited for it to heat. "When did you have time to make a casserole *and* chop wood? Did you even sleep at all?"

"I'm an early riser," he answered as he turned to leave. "I'm going to take a shower. I'll be back down by the time the casserole is done."

"He must get up at the butt crack of dawn," she mumbled and shivered her disgust of the idea. She'd drunk two cups of coffee before Dylan remerged and sauntered into the kitchen with wet hair and dressed in clean clothes. He grinned, and her heart melted a little more.

"So what are you going to do with the Heart when we find it?" Lily asked, serving up the plates and then sitting down across from him.

One brow rose in question. "It's not mine; it's yours. You own the house and the property."

She took a sip of her sweat tea. "Does that bother you?"

"That you own it?" He shrugged. "Well, it's been in my family for generations. I hope that if you ever sell, you'll give me first option to buy it back."

Lily smiled. "Deal, but only if you agree that the Heart is yours. It's your family's legacy. It was given to Henry to keep safe. So that makes it Sawyer property, an heirloom that you can pass down to your kids, much like the rocking chair."

"Lily...."

"No, I insist. If you want first option to buy this place back, then I insist that you keep the Heart as part of the deal. It was entrusted to your family."

"That's generous of you."

"It's only fair. So where do we start?"

Lily took a bite of the hash brown casserole and closed her eyes. A moan slipped by her lips as she chewed. The melted cheese was heaven in her mouth, and the ham was salty and complemented the veggies and eggs. Why hadn't she ever cooked this before?

She opened her eyes to find Dylan's lips parted, his fork up to his mouth and paused in mid-air. "I take it you don't hate it?"

She chuckled. That was the understatement of the year. "You should have been a chef instead of working security."

"I like to dabble in the kitchen. It helps relieve stress and keeps me out of trouble."

She smiled. "So what's first on the agenda for our adventure?"

He took a bite and swallowed before answering. "I figured we'd go through my dad's things and see if he left any clues."

"Clues would be good. Let's hope your old man was as anal about finding the treasure as you are about using the right spices."

"Let's hope."

Lily ate everything on her plate and helped do the dishes before they made their way to the attic. "You know if you continue to cook for me, I'm going to have to take up jogging, and I hate jogging."

"There are other ways to burn off calories." He glanced over his shoulder when he reached the top landing to the attic and grinned.

"Mind out of the gutter."

He chuckled and pushed the stubborn door open. "Swimming. I meant swimming, but let me know if you need a partner for the other."

"You're incorrigible," she teased as she tried to pass.

He stopped her, their bodies pressed together in the tight doorway. He ran his finger down her cheek while holding her gaze. "And you're beautiful when you're flustered."

Lily held her breath, afraid if she said a single word that he might release her, or worse, that he might stay where he was.

"I want to kiss you." His words came out a whisper. She felt the rapid beat of his heart pressed against her chest.

"Friends don't kiss."

His eyes searched hers, for what she didn't know. Seconds ticked by without either of them saying a word, nothing to break the spell he held her in.

He ran his fingers down her neck and her bare arm. His fingers toyed with hers. "Dylan….we…."

"Can't. I know." He eased away from her, moved inside, and stopped in the middle of the room.

Lily sighed through the sexual tension and entered behind him. Boxes on top of boxes lined the perimeter of the room. Memorabilia that didn't fit into a box stood around the room. A wooden chest, a toy horse, fishing poles, all kinds of odds and ends filled the space. "I can't believe it's all still here."

"My mom and aunts helped me label what we could by the rooms they came out of. There is more in the storage shed, along with the furniture." She glanced around the room. "I just didn't have the heart to get rid of any of it. I just couldn't."

He turned to meet her gaze and pulled her against his body. He lowered his head, and the next thing she knew, his lips were pressed against hers. His kiss wasn't passionate like it had been downstairs. It was sweet and inviting, and sincere.

He eased his lips away but didn't let her go. "Thank you."

He trailed a finger against her cheek, brushing her hair behind her ear, even though sadness clouded his eyes. "Thank you for not getting rid of it." He dropped his hand and stepped back, releasing a long breath. "I'll make plans to have everything moved out so that you can have the space back when we're done."

"Dylan...."

He turned his back to her and went to the wooden chest in the middle of the room. He dropped down to his knees and lifted the lid. "This chest was my mother's. My dad carved it for her as an anniversary present."

"It's beautiful," Lily replied as she walked up. She ran her fingers over the quilt inside the trunk. "And so is this."

He glanced up at her, a sad smile on his face as he pulled the quilt out. "That has been in our family for much longer. My grandmother made it with her bare hands. She was a stickler about this quilt. She wouldn't let any of us touch it if we had sticky, dirty hands." He pulled out the quilt and handed it to her. "She'd want you to have this."

Lily took the quilt and ran her fingers over the design. "Oh, I couldn't. She didn't even know me."

"She'd tell you, as she told my mother, that it belongs to the lady of the house as a reminder of the love that flows inside. It's said to have magical powers."

Lily grinned, and her eyes darted back to the quilt.

"What kind of powers?"

"It's believed that if you sleep under the blanket, you'll dream of your one true love."

Lily tried to hand him the blanket back. "I don't believe in magic."

"Suit yourself." He shrugged. "But you are still the woman of the house, so technically, it's still yours."

"She sounds like an interesting woman."

"She was," Dylan answered, continuing to look through the box.

"Where do you want me to start looking?"

Dylan glanced around the room and let out a hefty sigh. "He would have kept the information hidden, so I'd say either in his room or the boxes labeled Study."

They both went to work, looking through boxes; she was quicker than him. With every memento he touched, he'd pause, as if remembering something special. Her heart ached as she watched him; she could read the sorrow in his eyes and in the slump of his shoulders when he picked something up and closed his eyes. It was in every action, every movement, and in every item in the room. She knew the look; she'd worn the look when she'd gone through Joe's things. It had broken her heart and stolen her breath, and the memories were just as fresh as his loss had been.

She pulled a picture frame out from one of her boxes. It was a couple with a young boy around the age of twelve standing in front of them. She recognized Dylan instantly. The woman in the picture was pregnant.

"You were a cute kid."

Dylan's cheeks turned a bright red as he glanced at her. "I was a hellion."

"So, I was right." Her eyes widened in surprise.

"Partially," he admitted and started digging through his box again.

"Your mom was beautiful." Lily's brows dipped. "She was pregnant in this picture. Do you have any brothers or sisters?"

Dylan paused. "Yes and no," he answered. "I had a sister, but she died when she was five. She was in the same car accident as my mother."

"Oh Dylan, I'm sorry." That little girl had to be Mel. It made sense that she was still playing in the only house she knew as home.

"It was a long time ago."

Lily continued looking through the boxes and pulled out another picture, this one holding the little ghost that had appeared in Lily's room. She held up the picture. "Is this her?"

He smiled, got up, and walked over to the box. "Yeah. That's Melanie."

"Mel," Lily whispered.

Dylan cocked his head to look at her and took the picture out of her hands. "Mel," he repeated, not asking how she knew the nickname. "She hated her name. She was a tomboy at heart and liked for us to call her Mel."

"Sounds like my cousin, John's wife. Her name is Delaney, but she goes by Del."

"I bet she's a handful too," he replied.

"You have no idea," Lily answered. "Delaney kicked his ass when they first met. She stormed into town like a Tasmanian devil, and John was mesmerized, his plans changed on a dime. It's funny; they were also on a hunt of sorts, only their prize was a dagger, a picture, and putting her father behind bars."

"Let's hope luck runs in your family because it doesn't run in mine." He chuckled and went back to his box.

Lily's cell rang as she was searching. She pulled the phone out of her pocket and answered it.

"Why did I dream of you with a miner's light on your forehead?" her cousin John asked.

"I have no idea," she answered. "Maybe you're overworked and my dad needs to give you the day off?"

He chuckled. "How's the house guest? Is he still alive and sporting both kneecaps?"

Lily grinned. "He's been a perfect gentleman. Well, if you don't count when he tied me to the bed with rope, armed only with a feather."

The line went quiet, and Dylan's gaze swung to hers. His mouth was parted. She'd silenced them both with her superpower of words.

"I'm teasing, John. That's actually on the agenda for tomorrow."

"Lily Bennett," he admonished.

"I'm kidding. It's a joke."

"Hmm mmm. I'm glad you're joking again, but you can keep your sex life all to yourself. As far as I'm concerned, you're still that preteen that swears she'll never date."

Lily grinned at the memory and covered the phone. "That was a joke. Lighten up, Dylan."

"I hear Christopher stopped by."

Lily's smile slipped. "Yep. You can thank my mom for that one. Dylan played the part of boyfriend, but I nipped that in the bud too."

"Smart thinking, you don't want to get the aunts all giddy and making wedding plans, but the damage is done. Aunt Claire is having her annual Christmas Eve dinner tomorrow night. Your presence has been requested."

"Oh? So I have a choice?"

"Ha ha…You're smarter than that. The rest of the family wants to meet your house guest, so you need to bring him."

"And if I don't?"

"Bite your tongue. I'm not dealing with the aunts and their questions about him." She could hear the tease in John's voice. "Either you come to dinner or we're all coming to you. I hope you have enough food prepared to feed a gazillion of us."

"I'll be there," she answered.

"You'll both be there," he corrected.

"Have you always been this bossy and I just haven't noticed?"

"It's part of my charm. Make it happen or I'll send Uncle Mike to bring you by with the lights and sirens after he makes a slow trip down Main Street with the two of you in the back seat."

"You drive a hard bargain."

"The aunts like to get their way. Be sweet, Lily bug."

"When have you ever known me to be sweet?"

"When you were ten. I sure do miss that girl."

"Well, she's ancient history. Tell them I'll be there with bells on."

Lily hung up and pocketed her phone. She turned to find Dylan watching her.

"A rope and a feather? I can make that happen."

"That was a joke, but you know what's not a joke?"

He crossed his arms over his chest. "What's that?"

"Our presence is requested at my Aunt Claire's tomorrow for Christmas Eve dinner."

"Oh, I can't impose on a family dinner."

"Let me rephrase...your presence is *required* at Aunt Claire's tomorrow, so if you don't want a cop car coming to pick us up and taking the long way down Main Street, and I quote 'with lights and sirens' then you'll happily tag along as my plus one." Lily grinned and went back to working in her box.

"I haven't done a big Christmas Eve since"—he paused as if trying to remember something he'd forgotten—"the year my mom died."

"Well, then you're overdue."

"So it seems."

Lily replaced the items back into the box she'd been looking through and closed the lid. "Have you found anything yet?"

"No." He glanced at her. "You?"

She shrugged. "I haven't found anything that screams *look here,* if that's what you're asking, but then again, I don't know if anything is out of place either. He could have easily jotted down something, and what looks normal to me might look abnormal to you."

"Point taken," he answered and re-stuffed his box. "Have you noticed any large construction equipment on the property since you moved in?"

She grinned. "Yeah, by the old mining shafts on the north end of the property."

"We need a break," he announced while picking up two old minor headlamps. He walked over to her, put one on her head, and flicked the light on and off, making sure it worked.

"Why do I need this?" she asked, pulling it off her head and looking at the contraption.

"Because my dad bought equipment recently. I figure that's a good place to start looking until we have more to go on. You care to take a walk?"

Lily smiled. "Sounds perfect, but I hear those old shafts are full of ghosts."

He grabbed the other light and tossed his arm around Lily's shoulder. "You don't believe in ghosts, do you?"

How was she supposed to answer that? If she said yes, he'd think she was nuts. If she said no, then she'd be lying.

"Do you?" she countered.

He quirked his brow and smiled. "I believe it's possible they exist. What would we have to look forward to if they didn't?"

She was surprised by his response.

"Let me just grab some gear and a coat."

Dylan grabbed a backpack out of his room and led the way down the stairs into the kitchen. His backpack was similar to one she'd seen her father carry, one that had secret compartments. Was he armed? Considering his line of work, it wouldn't surprise her, but she didn't press for answers. He grabbed a couple bottles of water and stuffed them in the backpack, along with a few granola bars.

Lily shrugged into her jacket before sending a text to John to tell him where they were going, in the event, heaven forbid, they got stuck in one of the shafts. The idea of being in such a confined space with Dylan was enough to set her on edge, but if the shaft collapsed and their lights went out, she wasn't sure what she'd do. Take the opportunity to jump his bones under the cover of darkness or panic, worried they might run out of air? Maybe both.

She touched his arm and stopped him on the way to the door. "I'm not sure this is safe."

"We won't go in far, just far enough to get an idea of what good ole dad was up to, and then we'll get out. I'm just trying to get a feel for what was going through his head. It had to be something important for him to spend the money earmarked for his back taxes on that damn equipment."

Lily grabbed her own backpack and filled it with her gun, a small first aid kit, and a couple of roadside flares and spare batteries. If she was going underground, she wouldn't be staying in the dark. A shiver skirted down her spine.

They walked the two miles to the back of the property line where the mining shafts sat.

"Why did they originally build the mining shafts? Do you know what they were after?"

"Nah, I never really asked, but apparently it wasn't fruitful." Dylan glanced at Lily and grinned. "Or they wouldn't have had a mortgage on the house." He continued to lead the way through the thicker forest of trees, only stopping when they got to the property line. Voices carried on the wind to their ears. Apprehension engulfed her, and she stiffened in place. Dylan pulled Lily down and out of sight. As she peered through the leaves, there were two things she knew for certain. Ten strangers were trespassing on her property and they were carrying things into her mine and coming out empty-handed.

"Who do you think they are?" she asked, her voice a whisper.

"I don't know," he answered.

He gaze went to the little dirt path they must have entered on. She would have never considered using that path as a road.

She pulled out her phone and changed the ring tone to vibrate. She zoomed in as best she could and took pictures of the people and tried to get pictures of the tags on the trucks. She fired off a round of texts to her father and to John, telling them what she'd found and what she was about to do.

She pulled out her gun and put it in the waistband of her jeans. She handed the phone to Dylan and told him to stay put. She was up and out of arm's reach before he could stop her.

Lily strolled up to the men working, her gaze scanning the crowd to see if she could pinpoint the man in charge. She spotted him instantly. He was in a button-down shirt and a nice, thick, expensive jacket. She paused, just close enough so that she could talk but far enough away that he wouldn't be able to reach her. She gripped the gun in her waistband, her finger on the trigger.

"Excuse me," she hollered through the noise.

No one even noticed she was there.

She pulled out the gun and shot a round into the air. The sound had the men ducking and dropping to the ground out of harm's way. The only ones left standing were the head guy and her.

"I said excuse me," she repeated. "You're trespassing on private property."

The man's lips quirked at the corners. "Is that right, princess?"

"That's right, dipshit. I've called the law, and you've got two minutes to get the hell off my land before they get here."

A few of them exchanged glances, but the head guy remained unmoved.

"Now let's talk about this, sweetheart."

She levered the barrel of her gun at him. "You know what happened to the last asshole who called me sweetheart?" She raised her brow. "He walks with a limp."

The head guy moved around the truck to stand out in the open in front of her, as if taunting her to see if she had the guts to follow through on her promise. "Are you threatening me?"

"Yes, I guess I am. Do you know the law for trespassing in North Carolina? Because I do."

"At worst, it's a second degree misdemeanor," he answered.

She grinned. "That's true, but do you know anything about my town? Not only am I related to half the force, the other ones consider me an honorary daughter. Do you know what they'd do to a man like you for scaring their daughter?"

"You talk a big game, little girl."

She fired at an aluminum can at the rear of the truck. The impact sent the can flying in the air. "It's not all talk if I can deliver on my promise."

She quirked her brow and the guy still hadn't budged.

Within minutes, vehicles careened onto the property. Her uncles got out of the cars, guns in their hands, wearing extras in their holsters.

"What's the problem here, Lily?" John asked.

Uncle Mike's vehicle was the last to arrive, blue lights flashing and sirens wailing. He got out of the car, his badge hanging from his belt.

"Lily?"

"They're trespassing on private property."

"Do you have it visibly posted?"

Lily grinned and nodded. "Of course."

Mike walked over to the guy, and Lily lowered her gun. She glanced back at where Dylan was in the woods, and she spotted the barrel of a rifle trained on the guy she'd been talking to. Her brows dipped in confusion. She hadn't even known he'd been carrying.

John walked over to her and tossed his arm over her shoulders. "Where's your guest?"

"Twenty yards behind us, apparently covering my position."

John glanced behind him before watching Mike proceed with his interrogation. "You didn't give him a choice, did you?"

"Not really," she answered.

John gave a slow nod. "Well, at least he had your back. From the looks of his weapon, he was probably Special Forces, a sniper if I had to guess."

"He's just full of surprises," she announced and glanced back before turning around again.

John squeezed her shoulders a little tighter. "Next time, you might want to let him do all of the heavy lifting."

"There won't be a next time," she answered and left John's embrace, headed in the direction of her father. She explained what type of security and monitoring she wanted stationed around the property, so the next time someone broke the perimeter, she'd know. He agreed.

"Lily, do you want to press charges?" Mike called over his shoulder.

"Yes," she answered without hesitation. She pointed to the man in charge. "Only him. The others can go."

Mike shrugged and started reading the man his rights. He handcuffed the guy and stuffed him into the back of a patrol car before he rejoined her and her father.

"The guy says you shot at him."

Lily smiled. "Uncle Mike, if I had shot *at* him, he wouldn't be standing."

Mike nodded. "Good point, squirt. I'll question him when I get him in the office. Next time, wait until we get here before you instigate the assholes."

"I had backup." She pointed back to the tree line where Dylan was sitting up and disassembling his rifle.

The trucks the guys had driven in started pulling out, along with the cop car and her uncle's vehicles. John and her dad stayed behind, and they all walked over to where Dylan was waiting with his backpack shrugged over his shoulder.

"Good thing you came prepared, Dylan."

Dylan held out his hand and shook her father's. "Yes, sir."

John crossed his arms over his chest. "Special Forces?"

"Three years." Dylan nodded.

"Have you ever seen those guys before?" her dad asked.

"No, sir, but then again, I've been gone for a while."

John picked up one of the headlamps and handed it to Lily. "You'll need this."

"Thanks." She stuffed her gun back into her backpack. "It's time to explore, hotshot."

John rolled his eyes as he walked away.

She watched as John and her dad left. Dylan took a deep breath and turned to face Lily. "Are you nuts? Why in the hell would you do that? You didn't know I had a gun or that I could shoot. What if they'd jumped you! There were ten of them, and only one of you."

"Dylan, I have my secrets just like you have yours. Sniper, huh? Nice."

She tried to walk away, but he grabbed her arm, spinning her around to face him.

"And Joe? Would he have just let you walk into a threat like that?"

Lily narrowed her eyes. "How dare you? You don't know a thing about him or me."

"How dare I? Sweetheart, you have no idea how close I came to shooting that asshole. One more step toward you and it would have been his last. Did you even know that you had two targets on you?" He pointed up the mountain. "They were on the ridge at your two and ten. I might have been able to stop one, and if I'd been lucky, I would have gotten the other before you had a bullet through that thick skull of yours."

Lily turned and scanned the mountain, looking for any signs the gunmen were still around.

"They disappeared when the first car showed up in the distance and were probably long gone by the time your family ever got out of their cars."

Dylan's jaw ticked. His stiffened stance told her enough. He wasn't done yet. "Do you have a death wish? Is that what this is about?"

She remained quiet, not out of fear, but because she didn't know the answer. His face was heated, and the blood vessel at his neck throbbed. He was pissed, and she could read it in his eyes. He left her standing there and stormed off into the shaft.

Lily let her head fall back on her shoulders and raised her face to the sky. She'd overreacted and maybe jumped the gun by confronting the jerks without a plan. She was wrong, and it pained her to admit it.

She followed into the opening behind him and found him squatted down and unzipping one of the bags left behind by the trespassers.

"I'm sorry." Her voice echoed down the shaft.

He paused with his hands on the zipper before he rose. "I'm sorry too. You scared me, and I don't scare easily."

"I didn't like that they were here. I felt violated, and it pissed me off."

He cupped her cheek with his warm palm. "I know you don't need my protection, but, Lily, please think next time.

You were outnumbered, and we were outgunned. If anything would have happened to you...."

"It didn't." She hoped he could read the sincerity in her eyes. "I'll be smarter next time. I promise."

He held her gaze for seconds, his eyes searching hers as if trying to make her soul understand.

"I'm holding you to that." He dropped his hold and stepped back. He turned and pointed to the bags around the entrance. "Dynamite sticks, pick axes, and other mining equipment. It looks like they were setting up shop to start mining."

"What do you suppose they were after? They couldn't have known about the Heart."

A noise came from farther down the shaft. Knocks and then the sound of a moaning ghost. The moan was as fake as the ones she'd heard in ghost houses at Halloween. Ghosts talked in complete sentences, sometimes they made sense and other times they talked in riddles; so, whoever was down there was just trying to scare them away.

"Tommyknockers."

She chuckled. "A ghost that doesn't think we belong."

"I own this place, and we're not leaving," she yelled down the shaft. The knocks came again, only this time to the sound of the familiar shave and a haircut.

"Come on, let's call it a day. I think our nerves are shot from the crew that was here. Why don't we come back in the morning?"

She nodded, but she wasn't leaving because she was scared of a ghost of all things. She was leaving because she was strung tight, just like Dylan thought. She needed to relax, and standing around several bags of explosives only made her tenser.

She pulled out her phone and fired off a text.

"What are you doing?"

"Letting my dad know about the dynamite. He'll send his guys to get it when he's setting up my security."

Dylan tossed his arm around her shoulders and started walking out of the shaft. "Smart and beautiful. That's a deadly combination."

"I have my moments."

"I'd say so. How about we both take the night off from treasure hunting and I'll take you out to dinner."

7 CHAPTER

They both trekked back toward the house, and she paused when she noticed the familiar man in a chauffeur hat waiting next to the Town Car parked out front.

"Who is that?"

"Evelyn, Joe's mother."

Evelyn rounded the corner of the house, her coat pulled tightly around her body. The threads probably cost more than Lily had paid for her house. Her graying hair was styled short and in soft waves, her makeup perfectly applied, and the diamonds around her wrist and on her fingers glinted in the afternoon sun.

"Evelyn, I wasn't expecting you. Is everything all right?" Lily asked as she approached.

If Evelyn was curious about Dylan she didn't say anything in words, but she couldn't hide the way she looked down her nose. She cleared her throat. "Is this one of your cousins you've told us so much about?"

"No." She gestured to Dylan. "This is Dylan. He's....a friend."

"Oh, I see."

Lily waved her hand. "No...his father owned the house and...oh, forget it. It's a long story."

Evelyn wrapped her arm around Lily's. "You don't mind if I steal her away for a cup of tea, do you?"

"Of course not," he answered. "I still have a ton of my dad's boxes to look through up in the attic. I'll just leave you two to visit."

Evelyn's smile was pinched as she directed Lily toward the front door. He followed behind them and disappeared up the stairs and out of sight.

Evelyn walked farther into the room, her gaze assessing. "You didn't waste any time."

Evelyn's eyes rose up the staircase.

"Excuse me?"

She put the fake smile on her face and lifted her hands, gesturing toward the living room. "Oh, I didn't mean anything bad, darling. I mean, he's been gone six months, and in that time, you've quit your job, bought a house, moved, and now you've taken in....a what? Roommate?" Her last word dripped with disdain. "Lily, if you were hurting for money, you know all you had to do was ask. Joe would have never forgiven me and his father if we didn't take care of you."

Lily's mouth parted. Words failed her. Well... words that she could use that wouldn't alienate the woman who had given birth to her dead fiancé.

"Evelyn, are you suggesting that any of this has been easy for me? I lost the man I loved, the man I was going to grow old with. The man who was going to give me *your* grandchildren, so excuse me if you don't think I've grieved hard or long enough or if you can't tell because my face isn't stained with my tears." Lily stepped toward the older woman. "You know nothing about what it's been like for me." Lily crossed her arms over her chest. "Was there anything else you needed?"

Evelyn dropped her fake smile, and her eyes and face softened. "Lily...I didn't mean..."

Lily took a deep breath and exhaled. "Yes, you did, but it's okay." Lily rubbed Evelyn's arms. "I miss him, every day. Now how about I make you that cup of tea? I could use a cup of warm coffee myself."

They walked into the kitchen, and Lily started a kettle for the tea.

"I didn't mean to upset you, Lily. He'd want you to be happy."

"I know." Lily swallowed around the lump in her throat and finished making the tea and her coffee. Seeing Joe's mom brought back memories of better times gone by, and with it, the shame of how she'd acted with Dylan.

"Please sit, dear." Evelyn gestured toward the other chair. "I didn't come here just to check up on you. I came because there is something I need to tell you, and I'd rather you hear it from me."

Lily eased down into one of the chairs, suspicious of the way the conversation had turned.

"Tell me what?" Lily asked before sipping her coffee.

Evelyn cupped her hand around the teacup, not bothering to take a sip. "Do you remember when you and Joe decided to take a break a few years back?"

Lily leaned back in her chair. "How can I forget? We were both so young."

Evelyn cleared her throat and lifted her gaze to Lily's. "Well, during that break, you had both agreed to see other people. Isn't that right?"

Lily placed her coffee cup in front of her and crossed her arms on the table. "Yes."

"Well, I don't know if you dated other people, but Joe dated someone else during that time."

Lily swallowed hard and pressed her lips together. Joe hadn't told her he'd been with anyone during the time they were apart, but he was an attractive guy. It wasn't a far stretch to imagine he had. "Yes, well...we were split up. Evelyn, what are you getting at?"

"I don't know how to tell you this, dear."

"Just spit it out."

Evelyn took a deep breath. "After the funeral, a young lady and her son showed up on our doorstep."

Lily remained quiet, but her body went rigid.

"She said she saw the obituary in the newspaper."

Lily gave a slight nod, and her heart dropped into the pit of her stomach.

"She claimed Joe was her son's father."

Lily shook her head. "That's not possible. He would have told me. He wouldn't keep something like that a secret."

Evelyn's eyes told her that what she said wasn't the end of the story. There was more; she could read it in Evelyn's eyes, in the pity in which she stared back at Lily.

Lily's heart clenched.

"The little boy was the spitting image of Joe, but we had to be sure. We did DNA testing, and it was confirmed."

Lily shook her head. "He didn't know. He couldn't have known."

"That's what we thought, until the woman produced a picture of Joe and her son together. Not only that, but he'd started a trust fund for the child. He knew Lily. He knew."

Lily rose out of her chair and walked to the back door. She watched as the rays from the lowering sun danced on top of the pool water.

"I'm so sorry, Lily."

Lily clenched her eyes closed and lowered her head. Hurt and betrayal left her stunned.

Lily turned back to face the woman. "Why are you telling me this?"

"The trust fund."

"I don't understand." Lily took a step back toward the table but stopped. "What does the child's money have to do with me?"

"Joe listed you as co-owner on the trust." She pulled some paperwork out of her purse and pushed the documents toward where Lily had been sitting. "In order to reassign ownership, we need your signature."

Lily's mouth parted again. What the hell was she supposed to say to that?

"He must have been planning on telling you."

Anger welled up in her chest as she clenched her hands into fists. "When? When was he going to tell me, before or after we were married?"

Evelyn rose and slid her arms back into her jacket. "I don't know, Lily. I'm so sorry."

"It doesn't matter." Lily pressed her lips together, refusing to take her anger out on Joe's mom. She walked over to the drawer and pulled out a pen, signing all of the lines indicated by tabs.

"If you'll excuse me, I can't..."

"Yes, dear. I'll see myself out," Evelyn answered as she picked up the papers and stuffed them back into her purse.

Lily took her stairs two at a time, hurried into her room, and slammed the door behind her. She paced the length of the bedroom, back and forth, only stopping at the window to watch as Evelyn's vehicle pulled down the gravel driveway.

"I'm sorry." Joe spoke from behind her. "I never meant to hurt you."

Lily's face heated, his words, his apologies only adding fuel to her anger. She spun around to face the ghost. "How could you!"

"We weren't together."

Lily crossed her arms over her chest. "How could you not tell me? Did you think that I'd never find out?"

"Of course I wanted you to find out. That's why you were a co-owner. I just couldn't..."

"Couldn't what?" she asked through gritted teeth.

"I tried to tell you a thousand times, and each time I couldn't...find the right words."

Lily picked up the picture on her dresser and threw it at the see-through apparition. "You're a coward."

"I didn't want to lose you."

Lily tilted her head back to look up at the ceiling. "Did you honestly think I wouldn't understand?"

"We weren't together, Lily. I didn't know how you would react."

Lily met his gaze. Sadness replaced the anger she'd felt only moments ago. "You didn't really know me at all, did you?"

"Lily…."

"Just don't…" she started to say and was interrupted by a knock on her door.

"Lily?" Dylan's voice sounded from the other side.

"Just a second," she answered as she walked to the door and pulled it open.

Dylan's gaze darted past hers into the room where Joe was standing before it rested on her face. "How did your visit go? Are you okay?"

"I'm fine. Listen…do you care if I take a rain check on dinner tonight? I'm not feeling very well."

Dylan's brows dipped. "Sure." He rubbed her arms. "Let me know if you need anything."

"Thanks," she answered as she eased the door shut. She turned to find herself alone in her room. Just the way she wanted it. Just the way she needed it.

8 CHAPTER

Dylan went back into the attic and paused when he entered the room. The same ghost that had been standing in Lily's room was now hovering in the middle of the attic.

"You must be the infamous Joe."

"And you're Dylan."

"Are you here to scare me off from your fiancée? Because if you haven't noticed, I'm not going anywhere, and you're dead."

The ghost disappeared and reappeared seconds later, sitting on top of one of the boxes. "I've noticed. You like her?"

"Yes, not that it's any of your business. What did you do to piss her off? I could hear her yelling clear up here."

"My mother told her that I have a son."

Dylan planted his hands on his hips. "Why was that a shock? She was marrying you. Did she not like the kid?"

The ghost shook his head. "She didn't know."

Dylan dropped his hands to his sides. "Wow. That's a zinger of a secret. I can't blame her for being pissed."

"That's why I'm up here and not down there."

"I don't understand."

"You're doing the same thing. Don't you think it's time to come clean?"

"About what?"

"The call." Joe, the ghost, vanished and reappeared in a chair on the other side of the room. "Don't hurt her the way I did. It won't end well."

"Says the ghost with the secret love child."

"Says the man who loved her to the one she's destined to be with."

Joe, the ghost, disappeared from the room, leaving Dylan lost in thought. How had he gotten to this point in his life? He was in an attic looking for clues about something he wasn't sure even existed; and worse than that, he was talking to a man who loved the woman he was supposed to be with.

"They make movies out of this shit," he mumbled to himself and continued looking through more of the boxes where he thought he might find documents. He was emptying the last box when he saw a piece of paper sticking out of his dad's favorite book. Dylan lifted the book that his dad had read to him as a little boy, a story that Dylan knew well. The book was about a young boy on various adventures. Dylan eased the old leather binding open to where the paper was folded inside.

His dad's handwriting was scribbled across the sheet. "When you find her, never let her go. Enjoy every moment like it's your last. She owns the key."

"What key?" he questioned, no longer doubting that the stone was real.

Dylan rose from his spot next to the box, refolded the paper, and put it back where he'd found it. He put the book under his arm and strolled out of the attic. He paused by Lily's door. There were no sounds of sobbing coming from the other side. She was no longer talking to anyone either. Satisfied, he continued down the stairs and into the kitchen. The woman needed to eat, no matter how upset or mad she was. He was going to see that she ate.

Dylan went the simple route, with homemade soup and sandwiches. An hour later, he was holding a tray in one hand and using his other to rap against her door. "Lily, I brought you something to eat."

The door opened. Lily had already showered and changed into her PJ's. Her hair was pulled back in a ponytail and what little makeup she used on her face was gone, giving him a glimpse of the freckles that she hid on her cheeks. She was a natural beauty. He cleared his throat. "I made you dinner."

Her gaze went from his to the food and back. She stepped back, opening the door farther. "Have you ever been married, Dylan?"

He set the tray down on her nightstand and waited until she climbed up on her bed. "Yes."

Her mouth parted, and her brows dipped.

"Why do you ask?"

Lily shook her head as if clearing her thoughts. "Your actions." She gestured to the food. "You've got a kind heart. I bet you wouldn't keep secrets from the person you were going to marry."

Dylan shrugged. "I'm not perfect, Lily. I think we all make mistakes. It's part of being human. How we handle those mistakes and what we learn from them is what determines our character."

"My fiancé had a child and didn't tell me."

Dylan was waiting for the explanation that he'd already been warned about.

"I'm sure he would have told you about his son."

Lily paused with a piece of the sandwich up to her mouth. She set it back down. "I never said he had a son."

"I had a fifty-fifty chance of guessing correctly." Dylan sat down on Lily's bed and used his elbows to prop himself up. If she ever figured out how he knew, he'd have a lot more explaining to do then just him talking to her dead fiancé.

She handed him half the sandwich and one of the napkins he'd brought her.

"So you're mad he cheated on you? Or did he have this kid before you two met?"

"No," Lily corrected. "He didn't cheat. We were broken up when it happened. I'm mad he didn't tell me."

Dylan gave a slow nod. "Would it have changed anything if he had?"

Lily put the remainder of the sandwich down on the tray and slid off the bed. She crossed her arms over her chest. "No."

Dylan watched her, his gaze assessing. She was lying to herself. "You're lying."

Her hands dropped to her sides. "It wouldn't have changed my feelings, but yes, okay, yes. Are you happy I said it? I would have pushed him away to go be with his son and try and work things out with the mother of his child. I've seen what happens when you miss out on a child's life."

Dylan rose to stand in front of her. "You would have let go of the man you loved so that he could make his son happy?"

Lily's gaze dropped to the floor. He rested his palm on her arm. "Lily."

She didn't reply.

"You can't live in the what-ifs." He lifted her chin with the crook of his finger. "You have to live in the here and now."

Her face softened. "What are your secrets, Dylan?"

He pulled her against his chest and wrapped his arms around her body. He let the warmth of her body surround him. He couldn't answer her question, not yet. He kissed her forehead before stepping back and heading toward the door. He gave her a sad smile. "I'll tell you mine. The same day you're ready to tell me yours."

Dylan waited a split second before turning around and walking out and back to his room. He fell back on the bed, his eyes on the ceiling he'd memorized all of his life. What the hell was he doing? He had to tell her the truth, or this would end badly for both of them. There was no easy outcome, not with everything he'd kept from her already. She was going to hate him; it was inevitable.

A soft knock sounded on his door, and he slid off the bed to answer it. He pulled the door open, and Lily pushed her way into the room. Her arms wrapped around his neck, and her lips pressed to his in a kiss that melted his soul. He pulled her close, afraid to let her go. He might never get the chance to hold her like this again, not after he told her of the betrayal.

Her hands tightened around his neck, and she moved closer into his embrace. His head warred with his heart. His soul knew she was his, but she didn't. He broke the kiss, and his breath came out in pants as he stepped back putting some distance between them. "Lily?"

She shook her head. Her chest heaved. "Sorry, I, uh, don't know what came over me." She gestured over her shoulder to the door behind her.

Her words stung like cold water being doused over his head. She didn't want him. Not yet. "Did you think saying yes to me would make you feel better? Turnabout being fair play and all?"

Her lips pressed in a fine line, but she didn't deny why she'd been in his room. He stalked closer to her until her back was against the door. He caressed her cheek. The tip of his finger trailed down her neck. "When I take you to bed, I'll be the only man you're thinking about." He leaned down and kissed a trail along her neck where his fingers had just been. "The only man you want touching you..." He caressed her sides, resisting the urge to cup her breast. "Tasting you....teasing you." His words were a whisper on her skin as he kissed her neck back up the same path. He hovered before breaking the connection. "Then and only then will I take you to bed and spend hours worshiping your body the way you deserve. Not a moment before."

"Dylan..."

He rested his forehead against hers. "Please, Lily....don't test my resolve." He reached for her hand and placed it on the aching bulge in his jeans. "I'm not turning you away because I don't want you." He rubbed her hand down the length of him. "The problem is I want all of you, and I won't settle for less."

"I can't..." she replied and removed her hand. A tear trickled down her cheek.

"It's okay." He stepped back and watched her leave just as quickly as she'd entered.

Dylan ran his hand through his hair, pulling at the short strands. Not only his body, but also his heart, ached for her. This situation was one of the hardest he'd ever had in his life.

"Goodnight, Lily," he called after her, closing the door to his room.

9 CHAPTER

Lily's eyes slid open. Sometime in the night she'd succumbed to her exhaustion, and her mind had slowed. The sun streaming in through the open curtains heated the room and warmed her cheeks. She cringed from embarrassment, remembering her encounter with Dylan. Christmas Eve dinner at her Aunt Claire's house would be awkward unless she fixed the problem. He was her guest, and she'd practically begged him for sex. Lily pressed her eyes closed and rolled into her spare pillow in an attempt to muffle her scream.

A knock sounded on her door, and she rolled over.

"Lily," Dylan called from the other side of the door.

"Come in," she hollered back.

He opened the door and poked his head inside the room, his hand never leaving the doorknob. "I have to run into town and I'll be gone most of the day."

Lily sat up in the bed. "We should talk."

His lips eased into a small smile. "No need. We're good." He pushed off the door and walked into her room. He rested his hands on the mattress and leaned down, pressing a lingering kiss to her lips. "I promise; we're good."

"I'm embarrassed."

"Don't be."

"I shouldn't have..."

"You were hurt. I get it."

She lowered her head and picked at the invisible lint on her comforter. "It's no excuse."

"Lily, it's okay." The fine lines around his eyes softened, and he sat down on her bed. "I think it's time I came clean."

Lily raised a brow. It seems he had secrets too. "Oh?"

"I…" He started and then paused, his brows dipping as if he was debating the words he wanted to use. "We have chemistry, and as much as I'd love to explore it, I want more than just a physical relationship with you." He lifted his gaze to hold hers and rested his hand on top of hers. "I think we can have something real and lasting, and I'm willing to wait for it, to wait until you're ready, but there are some things you need to know about me…"

Lily's cell phone rang, and they both looked at it. "It can go to voicemail."

He shook his head and stood up from the bed. He picked up her phone and handed it to her. "Go ahead and answer it. We can finish this conversation later."

Lily opened the phone and sent the call to voicemail. "We'll finish the conversation now."

The phone started ringing again, just as Dylan was about to open his mouth. He gave her a sad smile and gestured to the phone. "It must be important."

She glanced at the caller ID and answered the call. "John, I'm busy..."

"Lily, he's lying to you."

Lily's gaze went up to meet Dylan's. "Give me just a sec," she said into the phone before covering the speaker with her hand. She slid out of the bed. "You're right. This is important. We can finish the conversation when you get back."

His gaze went to the phone and then came back to hers. "Who is that?"

"My cousin, John."

He slowly nodded. The smile he'd given her slipped into a frown. "Sure...I'll be back later." He leaned in and kissed her cheek one more time.

Lily waited until she heard the front door shut before she put the phone back to her ear. "Explain."

"I saw him....in my dream."

"Okay...what was he doing?"

"He owns an apartment above the Italian restaurant on Main. I saw him picking a suit out of the closet."

Lily eased to sit down on her bed. "You must be mistaken. He told me he always just stays with his father when he comes to town. He didn't have anywhere to go. That's why I let him stay."

"I'm sorry, Lily-bug, but I don't think he's being entirely honest with you."

Swallowing around the lump in her throat, Lily fell back onto the bed and pressed her lips together. John had to be wrong. *John better be wrong.* "Is that it? Is that all you saw?"

"I'm sure he had a good excuse. You know I get visions in my sleep, but there is normally more to the meaning than what I can see. Just be careful and ask him about it."

"I will. Thanks for calling."

"Don't forget about tonight. Should I assume he's still coming?"

"I guess that depends on what I find out," she answered. "I'll call you later."

She hung up the phone, no closer to having an answer for any of John's questions.

"Going to town," she mumbled beneath her breath. "I'll be gone all day," she continued.

Letting out a deep breath, she sat up. "What are you hiding, Dylan Sawyer?" She stood and walked into the bathroom, curiosity and anger heavy in her mind. "No more secrets...I swear if you lied to me...." she seethed and hurried through getting ready and grabbed her purse and keys on the way out of the door. John had seen the apartment in his dream; it was time to see just how accurate he'd been.

Lily parked across the street from the Italian restaurant right next to Dylan's motorcycle. Her heart clenched as she gazed up at the apartment above. A silhouette passed the window, a large man's silhouette. "Oh, Dylan," she whispered, her anger replaced with disappointment.

She glanced both ways before crossing the street and then rounded the corner of the building, looking for a back entrance or stairs up to the place. The thought of having to go into the restaurant and ask ate at her craw.

She found the stairs and made her way up. What if she'd been wrong? What if it was someone else? Her steps slowed as she reached the landing. She'd raised her hand to knock when the door opened. Dylan stood in the doorway. His eyes bulged, and his mouth parted.

"Lily...what are you doing here?"

Lily crossed her arms over her chest. "I can ask you the same thing." She tilted her head, fighting the range of emotions that ran through her. *Give him the benefit of the doubt, don't accuse*, she silently reminded herself.

Dylan stepped back and held the door open for Lily. She stepped into the room, and her gaze travelled over the sparse little space. The living room was small and had only a few places to sit. The television was old and included rabbit ears. She slowly turned, taking everything in, including the small kitchen that was connected. "Is this what you wanted to tell me?"

"Partially," he answered.

She swiveled to face him. Dylan ran his hand through his hair before dropping his hand to his side. "Care to sit?"

"No."

He took a step toward her, and she stepped back. "You told me you were going to stay with your father. Was that a lie?"

He shook his head. "No. I'd intended to stay with my dad. This place was just my sanctuary when I was younger, whenever I needed a place to get away. Rosa, the owner of the Italian restaurant, let me cook in her kitchen when I was younger."

"Is this place yours?"

Dylan's shoulders deflated. "Yes, but I hadn't planned to stay here. I'd told Rosa she could rent the place out if she needed to. I didn't know that she hadn't. After meeting your mom, I stopped by, and she told me that it was vacant. You'd already told me that I could stay."

Lily let out a breath she didn't know she'd been holding. "Why didn't you tell me?"

"I like you, Lily. I wanted to get to know you better. If you want me to move out, I will, but I'd really like to stay."

Lily let her arms drop to her side. "Is there anything else you omitted, anything else that I need to know?"

"Yes," he answered without hesitation. "But you might want to sit down for the rest."

"That good?" she asked as she walked over to the couch and sat down. Dylan sat on the coffee table in front of her. His gaze searched hers as he wet his lips.

"First, you have to promise to hear me out."

"Dy—"

He shook his head. "Promise that you'll hear me out."

Lily's heart clenched tighter then dropped into her stomach. Whatever he had to tell couldn't be good. "Fine. I promise."

He took her hands into his. His thumb stroked the top of her palm. "I guess I should start at the beginning."

Lily nodded.

"Growing up, I'd always been told the legend around the ruby was true. My grandfather was the first to tell me the story, then my father." He dropped his gaze to their locked hands. "I thought it was a myth. Something that the men and women in my family told me like an elaborate joke. I had no clue that it was real...." He looked up and held her gaze. "Until you."

Lily tilted her head, trying hard not to say anything until he was finished.

"They all tried to tell me that they heard the call. The voice of the woman meant to be theirs. Their soul mate." He stopped strumming his thumb on her finger. "I heard yours from across the sea. It started with crying. I knew you were hurt and you needed me, but I didn't know who you were."

Lily shook her head. "That doesn't...."

Dylan visibly swallowed. "Make sense?" he asked, finishing her statement. "No....it didn't. The ruby's legend says that the person you're destined to be with will call to you. In your dreams, in your waking day, it doesn't matter. The voice I hear is yours, Lily."

Lily's mouth parted. Words escaped her.

"It goes on to say that the ruby will draw the person you're destined to be with. It will be like a beacon to return home. My grandfather heard it; my father heard it; and now, I have too. I can't explain it. I don't know how it works. I just know I was meant to come home, and that you'd either already be here or be coming soon."

"You think we were destined to be together? That I bought your father's house because it was what...fate?"

Lily tried to stand, but he stopped her. "That's not all."

Lily rolled her head on her neck to loosen the knots in her shoulders. She sat back down and gave a silent nod. "Go on."

"I can see the ghosts in my...your house. I know you can see them too."

"Oh for the love of god." Lily tried to stand but was stopped short again.

"Tell me you can't," Dylan said as if waiting for her to admit the truth.

"I've...had the gift since I was little. But you..."

"The same," he answered without her even having to ask. "I think it's part of the legend. We're supposedly compatible in every way, like we were made for each other. The stone just makes it easier for us to find each other."

Lily leaned forward and rested her elbows on her knees. "You knew this and yet you married?"

"I thought it was a fairytale."

"What happens when we find the stone? Will it break whatever spell this is?"

Dylan shrugged. "I don't know that it is a spell."

She gave a slow nod. "Anything else that you need to tell me?"

"I'm...a millionaire," he said like a worried boy afraid of reprimand, and not the confident man she'd been living with.

Lily's gut clenched, not because Dylan was rich but because everything he told her was a lot to process.

"Any other secrets that might come out to bite you in the ass?"

He shook his head.

"Good." She let out a deep breath and rose. He rose with her, their bodies pressed together in the tight space between the couch and the table.

"Lily..."

She closed her eyes and gave a small shake of her head. "Dylan...this is too much...I need time."

"It's okay." He cupped her cheek.

She rested her hand on his chest, keeping the space between them. His heart raced beneath her palm. She drummed her fingers and then slid past him to the door. She walked out without looking back. Her mind was racing with the implications of what he'd said. What it meant. How was she supposed to process that he was her soul mate and he hadn't told her the truth from the beginning? Hell, she wouldn't have believed him.

Lily slowly walked down the stairs with her hand on the engraved rail, her mind in a haze. She made her way back across the street. She'd reached for her door handle when a hand landed on her shoulder.

"Miss Bennett."

She practically jumped and spun around. The man she'd had arrested for trespassing was standing right behind her.

He dropped his hand from her shoulder and stepped back. "I believe we got off on the wrong foot. I'm Waylon Sims."

Lily kept her thumb on the alarm button on her fob. "I don't care who you are. You were trespassing on private property."

Mr. Sims reached into his suit pocket and pulled out a folded document and handed it to her. "I had every right to be there. I had a contract with the previous owner that gave me permission, not only permission to mine the caves but also a year to buy that portion of the land. I didn't realize the previous owner was dead."

Lily opened the paper and scanned the contents. "How do I know that he signed this?"

"You can ask his attorney. He drew up the contract. You can keep that copy. I have the original."

"Regardless..." Lily folded the paper. "I own the property now, and you have no legal claim to be on it."

"Ms. Bennett. I've already got the explosion permits. I'm willing to sign another contract with you for double the price of the previous one if you'll give me permission to search the mine with the contingency to buy that portion of the land."

Lily tilted her head, her gaze studying the stranger that had snipers on the mountain. This guy was on crack. What miner brings hired guns to the property? Maybe a miner with worry someone would steal his bounty? "What are you searching for in the mine?"

"What does anyone search for in the mine?"

Lily opened her car door and was about to get in, but she turned around at the last minute. "Mr. Sims, that property is mine. I have no intention of selling the land or letting anyone else destroy it." She shoved the papers against his chest and paused. "And the next time you have snipers or guns on my property"—she narrowed her eyes—"will be your last."

"Call me when you change your mind." He pulled out a card and handed it to her before she climbed into her car. "Call me lucky, but I have a way of getting what I want."

"Stay off my property. Are we clear?"

Mr. Sims smirked. "Crystal."

Lily pulled out onto Main Street, her gaze in the rearview mirror. Mr. Sims was standing on the street with someone beside him, and they were watching her drive off.

Her phone rang as she pulled into her drive. She checked the caller ID and groaned. John was calling her again. She answered. "I don't care what you saw. I've had a long day, and I can't take any more."

"He fessed up?"

"You could say that," she announced as she got out of her car and stepped up onto her porch. She put the key in the knob and stilled. The door was partially ajar.

"Are you at the office?" she asked and removed her hand from the knob.

"Yes."

"Run a perimeter check on the property. I need to know of any movement in the last two hours."

"Lily, what's going on?"

"My door wasn't locked and is partially open."

"Wait outside. Do you understand?"

"I've got my gun. I'm going to do a quick sweep. I'm sure I just didn't pull it closed because I was upset earlier. My mom hasn't called, so I know I'm not in danger. Just call me back."

"Lil—"

Lily ended the call and shoved the phone in her pocket. She pulled her gun out of her purse and eased into the living room, her eyes scanning for anything out of place, anything out of the norm. She stepped slowly into the room. It looked exactly as she'd left it. Her gaze travelled to the rocking chair. The quilt that Dylan had given her, which she'd taken to her room, was now draped over the back of the rocking chair. "What?"

She stepped farther into the room, checking behind doors and in closets until the bottom level was cleared. She headed up the stairs, bypassing the creaky step as to not give away her presence. She eased the bathroom door open with her foot. Her hands trembled as she reached for the shower curtain and yanked it back. Her heart raced, expecting someone to jump out with a butcher knife clutched in their hand.

She continued down the hall. The next stop was Dylan's room. She hadn't seen it before he left and didn't know if anything was out of the ordinary, but she checked in all of the hiding spots she could find. Next was her room, and she did the same. The only thing out of the ordinary was the missing blanket that had been folded on her dresser.

She continued up to the attic, only pausing outside the door. She took a deep breath and opened it, the gun held out in front of her. The ghost of the little girl was sitting in the middle of the room, a set of jacks in front of her.

She held Lily's gaze. "I'm not in your room."

"I know." Lily walked throughout the room, making sure that no one was there. She turned back to Mel. "Has anyone been in the house today?"

"No...just the people who live here."

Lily leaned down to be eye level with Melanie. "I'll make you a deal."

"Sure," Melanie answered as she dropped the ball and scooped up two of the jacks in her little hand.

"You have permission to scare away anyone who doesn't belong, and if you do, I'll let you play in my room when I'm not home."

"Okay," Melanie answered without looking up.

"Do you know who moved the blanket downstairs and left it on the chair?"

Melanie caught the ball and looked up expectantly. "My mommy did. She said that you might need it."

"Oh well, that was nice of her," Lily answered and pushed to her feet. "If you see her again, I'd love to talk to her."

Melanie nodded. "I'll tell her."

"Thank you," Lily replied pulling out her phone and firing off a text to John letting him know that everything was okay.

Lily left the room and jogged back down the stairs. Her phone rang while still clutched in her hand.

"No point of entry on the property or in your house."

"Good to know," she answered and walked into the kitchen to put on a pot of coffee.

"So how did it go with Dylan?"

"It went," she answered without elaborating.

"Don't forget you two are expected at Aunt Claire's tonight."

That made Lily pause as she was reaching for a mug. "I'm not sure we'll make it."

"Wrong answer, Lily-bug."

"John, after the day I've had…."

"After the day you've had, you need your family. I'll come get you myself. Be ready in an hour."

10 CHAPTER

Dylan watched the exchange between Lily and the guy that had been at the mine. He reached for his gun the second he realized just who was talking to her. Just one wrong move and the asshole's tire would be flattened with a single shot.

Dylan lay with his belly pressed against the concrete balcony, his sight trained on the man that had threatened her just the day before. He couldn't hear the conversation, but he was an expert at reading body language.

His finger relaxed against the trigger as the man stepped back and out of Lily's personal space. Dylan kept his eye pressed to the scope until Lily drove off, only then lifting his head to look down on the trespasser when another man stepped out of the shadows.

Dylan pressed his eye back to the scope for a closer look. The guy looked scruffy with a five o'clock shadow. He wasn't wearing a jacket like a normal person; no, he had on a leather vest with a black tee-shirt beneath and jeans. Tattoos ran the length of his arm. The two looked like night and day. Was one the muscle, or maybe the sniper that had been on the mountain when Lily had confronted the men?

The man in the suit talked in hushed tones while the other guy nodded in understanding or agreement. They shook hands, and Dylan watched as the man in the suit disappeared into the truck that was waiting nearby and the hired gun stepped back into the shadows.

"Shit." Dylan rose and disassembled his rifle, stuffing it back into the special backpack he'd had designed for the piece.

Dylan hurried to the door and grabbed his motorcycle keys from the counter.

"Lily's in trouble." He opened the door and paused when he discovered three women standing on his stoop.

"No, she's not, but you are," Lily's mom, Emma, announced as she pushed her way into the small apartment, followed by Lily's Aunt Claire and another woman that he hadn't met.

"I would know," Emma continued. "You know Lily's Aunt Claire, but this is her other aunt that you haven't met, Abby, John's mom."

"I'm sorry. I was just on my way out."

"She's fine," Abby assured while checking her text messages. "John has assured me that he has eyes on the property." She looked up. "But you...on the other hand, don't have a clue."

"Excuse me?"

"What my dear sister means is that Lily is like a delicate flower. Under her hard exterior, she has feelings," Claire said.

"Feelings you hurt," Emma replied while narrowing her eyes.

"Don't do it again." Abby pulled out one of her guns and checked the barrel to make sure it was loaded before she put it back in her hiding spot.

"Ladies...I would never hurt her."

"We know you wouldn't intentionally," Claire acknowledged as she stepped farther into the room. She glanced out of the floor-length window that led to the balcony before turning back to face him. "You're screwing up, and we're here to help."

"Wait...how did you know?"

All three of the women grinned at the same time. "We just do," Emma followed Claire farther into the apartment and sat down on the sofa. "Lily is special."

He knew how special Lily was and not just what she meant to him. He knew her secret because he shared the same one.

"Perfect," Claire announced in a giddy voice as she clapped her hands. She turned to Emma and Abby. "He knows and can see ghosts too."

"Wait..."

An older lady's apparition appeared in the room. Dylan's breath caught as he took an unconscious step back. He kept his eyes trained on the intruder.

"You can see her," Emma said as more of a statement than a question.

Dylan's gaze swung to Emma. "You can too?"

Emma smiled. "I sure hope so. She's been taking care of Lily and me for as long as I can remember. This is Momma Mae."

"Yes, child," the apparition said. "I've visited your house. Those apparitions sure are stubborn. Now your mother, on the other hand...she could have easily been mistaken as one of the Bennett women."

"You've met my mother?"

"Oh yes, child. We just had a friendly chat at your house."

"He's got the gift?" Abby asked.

"I'd say so," Emma agreed.

"I don't understand," Dylan replied. "Why are you here and how is it possible that you know I screwed up?"

"Oh, that's easy, dear," Claire answered with a wave of her hand. "We're all gifted too. I can read minds; Emma can see ghosts and has an internal warning when a family member is in trouble, and Abby has the gift of psychometry."

"Psy what?"

"She can touch an object and get a read on where it's been and the past behind it."

"Is everyone in your family gifted?"

"Most of us, but that isn't the point. The point is... that you're losing her, and we're here to help you."

"How do you know I'm losing her?"

"John. He gets visions in his dreams. He saw the lie and he called to warn her."

"It wasn't a lie," Dylan corrected.

"Omission," Claire called out as she made her way into the kitchen and opened the fridge, peeking inside before turning around to address him. "You're a good man, Dylan Sawyer. Better still, you're the right man. Now don't screw it up any more than you already have."

Emma stood and moved to stand next to Abby at the door. "I assume you own a suit?"

"Yeah, but..."

"No buts. You accepted an invitation to dinner. We'll be expecting you," Claire patted him on the back when she passed him heading for the door.

"She's not ready for you yet, but she will be," Claire said. "Don't give up on her."

"All of the Bennett women have had difficulties with their soul mates. It's like a rite of passage or something," Emma said. "We were expecting the same for her."

"It's a good thing she's got us on her side. Don't screw up, kid," Abby announced as she opened the door and started down the stairs.

Emma followed. Claire paused with her hand on the knob. "We're expecting you in an hour, and we'll send a car to pick you up." She glanced around the apartment once more. "You won't be staying here. Your apartment is now officially under renovation."

"Wha…."

Claire winked. "I've already cleared it with Rosa, and she agrees that you're in need of a dire update. Don't worry; Lily won't let you sleep on the streets. It's not in her nature."

Claire pulled the door closed behind her, and Dylan could hear her whistle as her heels clicked down the metal stairs.

"What the hell just happened?" Dylan asked the now empty room.

"You've just been accepted into the family," Momma Mae chuckled. "You don't want to go up against those three. Trust me." Momma Mae let out a full- belly laugh as she started to dissipate out of the room.

Dylan grabbed a beer from the fridge. His mind swarmed with the new information. He walked out onto the balcony and took a long pull of the beer as he watched the sun setting behind the buildings across the street. Couples were still strolling along Main Street, hand in hand with packages dangling from their fingers. Kids were skateboarding down the sidewalk while some couples and families were entering Rosa's restaurant below. A man dressed in a Santa suit stood on the corner, the ding of his bell prompting passersby to stop and donate. His phone vibrated with a text from his attorney.

I think we found what we need. I'll be in contact.

Crap, that was something he'd forgotten to fess up about. He'd been looking to get his house back when he first arrived, and now, he didn't care one way or the other whose name the house was in, as long as the two of them were together.

Dylan fired a text back. *Stop all further action until we talk after the holidays.* He pushed all thoughts away. His only care was the woman who wasn't speaking to him.

He returned his gaze farther up the street and landed on the jewelry store across the way. A man was standing outside, peering in at the window display. How was he going to show Lily that they belonged together? Would a piece of jewelry work? He shook his head at the thought. "She needs something more." He let his gaze travel farther down the street. What could he do to prove himself?

His gaze landed on a car traveling down the road, a Christmas tree secured to the top. His thoughts were interrupted by a chime of another incoming text.

Quit lollygagging. Your ride arrives in forty-five minutes. ~Claire

I need to bail on dinner, so I can make things right with Lily. His fingers flew against the keyboard. *Can you tell her security that it's okay if I'm on the property, even though she won't be there? I've got a plan. I just need you to stall her from coming home and text me when she's on her way back.*

Sure. But you owe me. We will see you at New Year's.

Yes, ma'am.

That wasn't a question, dear.

****

John walked into Lily's house without bothering to knock on the front door. She wasn't surprised, but he would have been had she not expected him. He would have been looking down the barrel of the gun strapped to her leg beneath her long gown.

"You ready, slick?" John asked by way of greeting.

"I have to warn you," she answered as she rose. "I'm not in a very festive mood."

"Tell me about it in the car. We're going to be late."

Lily locked up and followed behind John. She slid into the front seat. "Where's Delaney?"

"She's already at Claire's."

"I could have driven myself. You didn't have to come get me."

"I figured it would give us a chance to talk. So start spilling. You've got fifteen minutes to tell me what the heck is going on." He started the car and backed down her driveway.

"He believes I'm his soul mate," she whispered.

John glanced at her before throwing the car into drive. "That was fast. You haven't known him, what, a week?"

Lily shrugged. "Less actually," she answered and turned to face John. "But what's even weirder is I kind of already knew, without him telling me. How strange is that?"

She righted herself in the seat, and her gaze went out to the passing tree.

"Weird for normal people or weird for our family? That has two different meanings."

Lily grinned for the first time since leaving Dylan at the apartment.

"If he feels it, and you do too, then what's the holdup? Did he explain the apartment?"

"Yeah....that and more." Lily's smile faded into a frown. How was she supposed to process everything he'd told her when she doubted he was telling her the truth? She didn't hear any call. She'd never heard of the legend that went with the ruby other than the pirate story from long ago. Was it possible?

Christmas lights were strung on most of the houses they passed. Tree lights twinkled through the windows in some of the houses. Tonight was supposed to be magical, and yet it was just another night to her. She hadn't bought a single present for her family or friends. She'd had an excuse, of course, with the move and Joe's death. Her heart ached for something, but she just didn't know for what.

"What are you going to do?"

Lily shrugged. "I don't know. I just lost Joe." She glanced at John. "And if what he said is true....does it mean that I was about to marry the wrong man? Not to mention that Dylan has already been married and he knew that it was the wrong woman."

"Some people just don't want to be alone. Did you ask him about his first marriage?"

"I'm not sure it's any of my business."

"When has that ever stopped you?" John chuckled and glanced over at her as he pulled down Claire's drive. He parked the car in front of Aunt Claire's big, decorated house and turned off the ignition. "If there's one thing that I'd learned when I found Delaney, it is that a love like that only comes along once in a lifetime. You need to seize the moment and make every minute count. Don't make the mistake I made. When she was stabbed, it just about killed me. The thought of living...."

Lily turned toward John. "I know...an experience like that has a way of changing your life. I saw it in you."

"Take a chance, squirt. Let the cards fall where they may."

"But he didn't tell me about the apartment."

John smiled. "I wouldn't have either, especially if it meant that I could spend more time with the person I wanted to get to know."

Lily playfully smacked John's arm. "You're picking his side?"

"I want what's best for you. If you need more time, just be honest and tell him that, but don't let fear stand in your way."

Lily let John's words settle into her mind and her heart. He was right. "Thanks, John."

"You're welcome. Now, can we go in and eat?"

"Sure," she answered and followed John out of the car, dreading the questions she knew her mom and aunts would ask about Dylan. John tossed his arm around her shoulder and led the way into the house.

He leaned into her and whispered in her ear, "Stick with me. I'll run interference."

"As if that's possible."

Dinner went by amazingly smooth. Only a few questions were asked by her mom and the aunts, but her mind was elsewhere the entire night. The festive decorations and easy banter did little to settle her thoughts, yet every time she'd tried to excuse herself to leave, Aunt Claire came up with another reason Lily needed to stay. Almost three hours later, Lily was finally released from captivity and was being driven home in the back of one of Aunt Claire's luxury cars.

The car had turned down her drive when lights caught her eyes. She leaned forward to tell the driver he'd made a wrong turn and paused when she realized that he was indeed at the right house. She leaned back in her seat, her gaze pinned on the view outside of her tinted windows. The car stopped, and the driver opened the door. She stepped out and admired the beauty around her.

She hadn't found time to decorate, and she'd yet to see the possibilities and beauty that the house could offer when fully decorated. A beautiful wreath made from garland hung on the door, her porch sparkled with little lights, and a line of poinsettias had been strategically placed. Candles in the windows were lit and welcomed her home. Smoke rose from the chimney. The house could grace the front of postcards, the scene so picture-perfect. The only thing missing was snow.

She walked to the door and turned the knob, not sure what she'd find.

"Surprise," Dylan announced and gestured to the room with open hands. Her banister was strung with green garland and tinsel. A Christmas tree stood in the corner, fully decorated. A train track was hooked up with the locomotive moving around the skirt. She let her gaze soak in all Dylan's decorations.

"Where..."

Dylan dropped his hands and smiled. "Some were in the attic, and the other things I bought from the store."

"I didn't have time."

"I know. I wanted to surprise you. I hope that's okay."

Lily set her purse down on the table just inside the door and walked farther into the room. "Dylan..."

He cupped her cheek. His gaze searched hers. "Lily...I know I dropped a bomb on you this afternoon, but I need to make one thing clear."

Lily leaned into the heat of his palm, savoring the feel of his touch. "What's that?"

"We'll take things slow, and I'll wait for you as long as it takes. I just want to be a part of your life and show you how right we can be together."

The ice around Lily's heart started to melt in that moment. She couldn't remember the reason why she shouldn't or couldn't be with him. "Spending time I can do, but soul mates..."

He smiled, and her sentence trailed off.

"It's a little too much to take in. I get it." He lifted her hand and placed it over her heart. "Joe will always have a place in your heart, and I get that, but I'm willing to bet, in time, there will be room for me too."

Emotions bombarded her with the force of a brick to the head. Hearing Joe's name, she felt guilty that she could feel this kind of pull to someone other than him. John's advice sounded in her mind. Yes, she loved Joe, but was she willing to walk away from the one man that could make her happy if the prophecy was right? She couldn't. She wouldn't. Joe would want this for her as much as she wanted it for herself.

Lily smiled up at him. "I'd like that too." The words should have been sour leaving her mouth, but they weren't. They were comforting, and oh, so right. She felt them in her heart, regardless of whether it was too much too soon. Slow and steady, she'd see where they would lead.

"Really?" His brows rose. "You mean it?"

Her smile grew bigger. "Depends."

"On what?"

"What other surprises you have in store," she teased.

He wrapped his arms around her and pulled her body flush with his. "How does popcorn and movies sound while we try and stay up all night to catch Santa?"

Lily chuckled. "I quit trying to catch Santa when I was nine, but the movies and popcorn sound great."

He pressed his lips against hers in a soft kiss. "Maybe a make-out session on the couch."

"You better keep it PG, mister. We wouldn't want to scare off Santa or be added to the naughty list," she whispered against his lips.

"I'm willing to take the risk if you are."

"Slow isn't in your vocabulary, is it?"

He pressed another quick kiss to her lips before tossing his arms around her shoulders and guiding her to the stairs. "I'll be a perfect gentleman. Now go change into something comfortable while I start the popcorn."

Lily jogged up the stairs and into her room. She closed the door and leaned against the wood. Her heart was racing. Was she doing this, really doing this? Her heart beat with more vigor than she remembered in a long time. The butterflies in her belly took flight.

"I shouldn't want this," she whispered to herself.

Joe materialized in the middle of her room. "You deserve to be happy."

"Do I?" She stepped closer to the apparition. "It's not fair. It was supposed to be you and me. How can I have these feelings for a man who isn't you? It doesn't make sense."

"Oh, Lily, love doesn't make sense."

Lily's mouth parted. "I never said I loved him."

"Not yet, but you will. Don't let my memory ruin that moment." Joe raised his see-through hand as if to cup her cheek. "I'll love you forever, Lily, but you need to live, and up until Dylan, you've been barely surviving. Be happy, smile, laugh, and revel in the possibilities. I want that for you. No more guilt, no more tears, no more sadness."

Lily shook her head. There were no unshed tears, no longer a feeling that her heart would shatter. She wanted those things for herself too. "I'll try."

Joe's lips split into a smile, and he dropped his hand. "You're going to be okay. It's time for me to go."

She nodded, knowing what he said was true. "Goodbye, Joe."

He winked as he dissipated out of sight.

11 CHAPTER

Dylan released a breath he hadn't realized he'd been holding. Lily hadn't kicked him out, just the opposite. He walked into the kitchen and started the popcorn before running up the stairs to grab some pillows and his comforter. He carried everything downstairs. After moving the coffee table out of the way, he positioned the covers in front of the couch, the pillows propped up so they'd have something to lean on. He popped one of the DVDs in the player, and as he was about to sit down, he spotted the quilt that he'd given Lily.

He grabbed it from the chair, spread it out, climbed beneath it, and waited for her return.

Lily stood at the top of the stairs after changing. She was looking down on him.

"You look comfortable."

"I will be when you join me."

She smiled and pointed down to the little nest he'd made them. "I never noticed the design on the blanket until now, it kind of looks like a house," she answered as she trotted down the steps and climbed beneath the blanket. He tossed his arm around her shoulders, and she snuggled into his embrace.

"Joe appeared in my room."

His fingers that had been stroking her arm stilled. "Oh?"

She looked up at him. There were no tear stains or watery eyes to indicate she'd been crying or in the least upset.

"He came to say goodbye."

Dylan's brows dipped, unsure he'd heard her correctly. "As in forever?"

She shrugged. "That would be my guess."

"So he's okay...with us, being together?"

Lily got up on her knees and climbed over his legs, straddling his lap. "He wants me to be happy," she answered as she leaned in to place a tender kiss on his lips. "And right now, you make me happy."

"Good to know." He held her at the waist, not wanting to ruin the moment when all he really wanted to do was make love to her. Right here, right now.

She ground down against his lap and moved her kisses across his cheek to his neck.

"Lily..."

"Hmmm," she answered against his neck.

"If you keep that up, I have to warn you...we'll be skipping PG-13 and heading right into rated-R and your name will be on the naughty list."

She placed one more kiss on his neck and trailed a path with her finger to his chest as she leaned up.

Lily grabbed the hem of her shirt and lifted it up and over her head, letting the material slip from her fingers to the floor. "I don't mind being on the naughty list if you don't."

He didn't wait for an invitation. He lifted his hips, letting her feel just how hard and naughty she made him feel, his cock straining against the material of his pants. He felt the heat of her core through the material, and it enflamed him even more. He reached behind her and unhooked her bra, easing it down her arms.

"This is much better than DVDs." His gaze devoured her perfect figure, his hands coming up to cup her breasts, the ivory skin beckoning to be touched. She felt like silk under his fingertips.

Her chuckle turned into a gasp as he lowered his head and latched onto a nipple, stroking the pebble with his tongue. His teeth gently tugged at the tip, making her legs tighten around him as she pressed down farther against his lap, rubbing against the hard shaft trapped between them. The scent of her arousal filled the air, pushing him to take more of what he wanted. Her.

"Oh, Dylan..."

Dylan didn't respond. Couldn't respond. The perfect weight of her breast in his hand was distraction enough, but the sweet sounds she made as he teased her nipple made him nearly mindless with pleasure. He turned to the other side, taking the dusky tip in his mouth and drawing on it long and hard, the distended tip just begging for attention.

Lily's head was tilted back on her shoulders as she leaned closer into his embrace. He wanted to feel her. He wanted to taste every inch of her, and yet clothes still separated their bodies. He need more from her. Wanted all of her. Even if he wanted to stop, he wasn't certain he could. Never had he desired a woman as much as he wanted her.

He released his hold. "I need you naked."

She raised her head and gave him a saucy smile as she stood above him. Lily lowered her yoga pants and panties until she could step out of them. As she stood above him, completely bare to his eyes, he saw the power lurking in her eyes, as if she knew he would do anything she asked. He reached for her, unable to resist, his hand curling around her hip. Dylan pulled her close, his nose brushing against the soft skin of her belly, his lips softly caressing her. His fingers parted the curls at the junction of her thighs, stroking her wet heat and finding the hard bundle of nerves that he desperately wanted to play with.

Dylan pulled his hand back and licked her cream off his fingers, his gaze boring into hers. Nudging her legs farther apart with his hands, he held her open, his tongue sliding through her juices, gathering them on his tongue like nectar. She tasted sweet, and he wanted more. He circled her clit, feeling the tremors run through her body as he teased her. Dylan knew what she wanted, what she needed, but she was going to have to beg him for it.

Soft noises slipped past Lily's lips as his mouth closed over her clit. He sucked the nub, lashing it with his tongue. Her hips bucked as she sought release. Unable to resist, he circled her opening with his fingers, easing first one, then another into her tight channel. Her silken walls clasped the digits, greedily sucking them in. He pumped them slowly, wanting to draw out her pleasure.

Lily moaned and grabbed his shoulders. Her legs trembled.

"I won't let you fall," he whispered against her. "I'll never let you fall."

He swirled his tongue against her clit again, his fingers plunging deep within her. Her pussy spasmed as she neared her first orgasm. Long, slow, deep strokes were building the fire within her slowly.

Her groans grew louder, her hands sliding into his hair, gripping it tightly. "Oh god."

Dylan moved his fingers in and out of her faster, harder. He needed her release, wanted to feel her pleasure on his tongue as she came screaming his name. And scream she would. Taking her clit between his teeth, he rapidly flicked the bud with this tongue as he hooked his fingers, stroking her sweet spot.

A scream bubbled out of her throat as she bucked against him. His fingers continued to stroke her, drawing out her orgasm.

"Dylan." The muscles in her legs flexed, her breathing labored. "Oh…my….I-I can't."

"You can, and you will."

Just as her first orgasm began to fade, he began stoking the fires again, relentlessly stroking, licking, sucking, driving her passion higher and higher. His fingers were slick with her cream, his cock pulsing in his pants. He felt her channel tighten around him a moment before she screamed out his name.

"Dylan!" He felt the little aftershocks in her pussy as her legs gave out and she sagged against him.

Withdrawing his fingers, he used his tongue to lap up all of her cream, wanting the fruits of his labor. Her taste exploded on his tongue as he drank her down. As his tongue stroked her wet folds, he savored the taste of the woman he was meant to love for the rest of his life.

"That wasn't fair." She grinned, got down on her knees, and pulled at his track pants, not stopping until his legs were free.

"Condom," he croaked then cleared his throat. "It's in my wallet."

Lily pulled out the condom, tore the wrapper, and slid the latex down his straining cock. She straddled his lap and eased down on top of him, guiding him inside of her.

His cock was so hard he ached, and he couldn't stop the groan that rumbled out of him as her wet heat encased him, taking him deep. He took several deep breaths so he wouldn't explode within seconds of being inside of her, his hands fisting at his sides in an effort to gain control over himself. Hell, if it felt this damn good with a layer between them, he didn't think he'd survive skin on skin.

She smiled and held his gaze as she raised herself before sliding back down. Dylan gripped her waist, afraid to let her go, terrified she might stop. As her ass touched his thighs, he thrust up, going deeper. She felt incredible, too incredible.

He squeezed his eyes closed and let his head drop against the couch. "I'm not going to last..."

"That's the point."

She giggled and moved quicker, rising and falling, up and down, over and over. Dylan reached between them, stroking her clit, not wanting to finish before her. He felt her tighten around him, squeezing, and he knew at that moment there was no way he was going to be able to hold out. Her body demanded satisfaction, and he'd be damned if he didn't give it to her.

"Next time, slower. I want to taste every inch of you. I want to be in you for hours, worship..."

He never got to finish his sentence. His balls drew up tight, his cock jerked, and then he was coming. He thrust a few more times as his seed filled the condom, triggering her orgasm, and he knew he would always remember this moment, this feeling of being with her for the first time.

She collapsed against his chest, her warm, slick body pressed tightly against his. Her panting breath slowed to a normal state. Dylan wrapped his arms around her, kissing her before he cupped her cheek.

"God, you're beautiful." He pressed his lips to hers. "That was amazing."

"You're amazing. Merry Christmas."

"The first of many." He grinned.

"Let's settle for the here and now. How about we shower and watch our movie?"

"Absolutely," he answered without hesitation. He carried her upstairs to her bathroom. He'd had a taste of her, and he wanted more. Their quick shower turned into all of the hot water turning cold, which turned into a thirty-minute process of dressing again before they made it back downstairs to start the movie.

Lily lay against his chest, her eyes closed from exhaustion. Everything was right in his world, for the first time in well...forever.

****

A loud explosion jolted Lily out of a sound sleep. Her dining room chandelier shook from the vibration. Dylan rolled with her, covering her body with his and covering her head. "Stay down."

The ground stilled, and he eased off of her, he gazed up to the ceiling before he got up off of her and held out his hand.

"What the hell was that?"

"Sounded like explosives," he answered as he looked around the room.

His gaze shot to hers, and his eyes widened at the same time it dawned on her what it could have been.

"The mine," they said in unison.

Lily's gaze darted around the room as she looked for her shoes while he threw on jeans and shoved his feet into his boots. She grabbed her phone and dialed John, hoping he might be at the office even though she knew he probably wasn't. He answered with a raspy voice and her hope diminished that he'd seen the culprit responsible. Her stomach twisted in knots.

"There was an explosion and I think it came from the mountain."

"Let me call in to see who was working. Stay put," John barked as he hung up on her.

Lily hurried through getting dressed. She had her coat on, her phone clutched in her hand, and her gun out and ready when her phone rang again.

"Is Dylan with you?" John asked.

"Yeah," she answered.

"Put him on."

"John..."

"I said put him on the phone, Lily."

Lily pressed her lips together and tightened her hold on the phone. Whatever he couldn't tell her had to be bad. She held out the phone to Dylan. "He wants to talk to you."

Dylan shoved the clip back in his gun before shoving it in the waistband of his jeans.

"Hello."

Dylan walked to the light switch and killed the light before heading to the front window and peering out of the curtains. "Yeah, Two...no...four."

Dylan stormed past her into the kitchen before returning to peer out the window again. "None in the back and the ones out front aren't on her property. They're on the main road. Yeah I agree," Dylan said without elaborating on what was going on. "We'll sit tight until you guys get here."

"Like hell we will," Lily said through gritted teeth. She placed her hand on her hip.

"Don't worry; I'll keep her inside if I have to tie her to a chair." Dylan hit the end button and handed her back the phone.

"What the hell is going on?"

"The explosion came from the mountain, but after checking the video, John tells me it didn't come through the mine entrance. They might be trying to tunnel in from another way. There are four guys outside. They aren't breaking the law unless they're some sick stalkers with a death wish, but it's better to be safe than sorry. John can't get a good look at them in order to figure out who they are. He can just see their vehicles and silhouettes. They are sending out a cop to get the guys to leave so we can go take a look at the mine."

Dylan cupped her cheek. "I'm sorry, Lily, but the explosion on the mountain sent boulders down and caved in the entrance to the mine."

Lily's heart dropped into her stomach. She hadn't even gotten a chance to explore the mine, much less look for the ruby.

Dylan pulled her into his embrace and kissed the top of her head. "Don't worry, Lily, we'll get these guys."

"I'm not worried about them. I'm disappointed we won't be able to find the ruby for you. We didn't even get a chance to look."

"Maybe the ruby isn't meant to be found." He tilted her chin up to look him in the eyes. "I don't care if we ever find it. I know it's real. You're my proof."

Lily stepped out of Dylan's embrace and headed toward the window to peek outside. The darkness of night cloaked their faces. She let the curtain fall back into place. "You can't expect me to sit here and do nothing."

"I can think of lots of ways to keep you occupied," he teased as he stalked her with a grin on his face.

With each step he took forward, she took one back until her back was against the wall. "Oh no, you don't."

Dylan wiggled his brows. "Oh yes...I do."

He trapped her in place with his hands on the wall. He leaned in, and she closed her eyes in anticipation.

The doorbell rang, and she opened her eyes as Dylan pressed a quick kiss to her lips. "The cavalry has arrived."

Lily went to open the door, but Dylan stopped her and tried to move in front of her. She nudged him out of the way and rolled her eyes. "You and I are going to have to talk about your caveman tendencies."

She pulled the door open and was greeted by her Uncle Mike and her cousin, John, standing on the stoop. "The people on the road were just high school kids looking for a quiet place to park and drink beer."

"Did you tell them I own a gun?"

Mike chuckled. "I put the fear of God in them, but I seem to recall catching you a time or two down at the lake with your friends doing the same thing."

Lily raised her hand to her chest. "You must be mistaken. I would never..."

"Oh please, Lily. You might be able to fool your parents, but you could never fool me." John gestured to her arm. "That watch has GPS in it. We kept tabs."

Lily planted her balled fist on her hip. "We only stopped hanging out there because of the bears, but...." She wiggled her wrist with the watch on it. "Now I just feel violated."

"Suck it up, buttercup," John said with a wink. "Come on, I'll drive you around to the mine so you can assess the damage. It's a good thing that mountain isn't closer, or I'd be worried about your house."

Lily grabbed her keys and locked the door before hopping into John's SUV. Mike had Dylan ride with him, and she could only guess what they'd be talking about. They wound around the property following the same small road the other guys had used to gain access to the mountain. Lily relaxed against the headrest. She watched the clock on the radio strike two in the morning. The evening air was chilly. "Shouldn't you be home putting together a Barbie house or something?"

"Barbie?" John asked as he glanced her way. "Have you forgotten who her mother is? I'd been testing out the latest ninja set, along with her first set of plastic throwing stars."

Who was Lily to judge? It made sense. Chloe was the product of her parents. John's wife, Delany, was the daughter of a mob boss, and John had been accepted into the FBI and was top of his class before he turned down the position to stay in Southall with Delaney. Chloe, was a Bennett, too, and gifted with even stronger talents like protective bubbles and telepathy just to name a few. She was stronger in one pinky than the rest of them combined. "I'm sorry to pull you away tonight."

He shrugged. "They were all sleeping anyway. I'd just finished wrapping gifts and had fallen asleep in the recliner when you called."

She nodded and turned back to watch through the passing trees outside.

"So how much of the mountain do you own?" He glanced her way. "Do you know?"

Lily shrugged. "I just know the mines. I never really looked at the schematics to see where my property line extends. It's not like I'm going to be climbing these big suckers."

"Might be something you need to do to keep these guys out."

"I'll see if we have the plans for the house and property when we get back to the house. I remember seeing them somewhere."

"It not, we'll have to get them from the property appraiser. I'm sure my mom could call in a favor."

"Oh, I wouldn't ask her to do that."

"You wouldn't have to ask. She'd do it in a heartbeat." He glanced over to her. "You know, it's too bad you don't have anything of the pirate's that you can let my mom hold and use her gift on. She might be able to help with that, too, by getting a read on the object."

"That would have been too easy." Lily smiled as John pulled up to the mine. She got out of the SUV and balled her fists, letting her fingernails dig into her palms as she walked closer, surveying the damage that was done. It wasn't fair. These men had come out of nowhere wanting whatever was hidden in the mine. It was time she dealt with them once and for all.

"Mike, who are these guys?"

Mike placed his palm on her shoulder. "Now don't go jumping the gun, Lily. I'll send a team out to the lake house to interrogate them, but until we have some concrete proof, we don't know that they're the ones responsible."

"Sure we do. Who else could want whatever is in there?"

"Who's to say there is something in there?" Dylan asked while crossing his arms over his chest. He scratched at his five o'clock shadow.

"Regardless, this is my property, and I think it's about time we took the offensive with these guys." Lily walked closer to the boulders, picked up a rock, and threw it toward the trees.

"I think I know just the people who can help me." Lily grinned and turned around to walk back to the SUV. She had one of Dylan's ancestors to conjure to scare the treasure seekers away.

"Where are these jerks staying?" she called out without turning around.

"They're renting the Miller's old lake house."

Dylan jogged up behind her and stopped her from getting in the SUV. "What do you have in mind?"

"First, I've got to make a call for reinforcements, and then I'm going to scare them out of town." Lily grinned. "And it just so happens, the person I need is already in town for the holidays and I ate Christmas dinner with her."

Mike walked over to the car, a bigger smile on his face then Lily's. "You wouldn't."

"Oh." She nodded. "I would."

John tossed his arm around Lily's shoulders. "Aunt Lydia."

Dylan glanced between them. "She has another aunt I haven't met? What's this one capable of if the others can read minds, predict trouble, and read objects?"

Lily's eyes bulged as she quickly glanced at John before looking back. "You know about us?"

"Your mom and aunts dropped by my apartment. They filled me in. So what can your Aunt Lydia do?"

"She can blow shit up and screw with emotions, and that's just for starters."

"Let's not forget her visions," Mike added.

John patted Dylan on the back. "Let's just say, she's not one you want to mess with." John crossed his arms over his chest. "You know, we could call in General Lister, and he could make them all just....go away."

Lily rubbed her hands together, a plan forming in her mind. "We'll use that as a last resort."

"We're all expected at Claire's tomorrow for dinner. How about we strategize then?"

"That sounds great," Lily answered.

"Bring the blueprints of your house and the land," John suggested. "I'd like to get a closer look at where your property line lays."

Dylan opened the car door and Lily slid inside. "That should be easy enough. I think they're in my dad's boxes from the library up in the attic."

Lily yawned as Dylan shut the door. She watched as the three talked for another minute before they got back into the vehicles and started a caravan toward her house. Even with the excitement of the night, she could barely keep her eyes open.

12 CHAPTER

Lily rolled to snuggle against the warm body next to her. She missed the feel of a man holding her tight. She snuggled in a bit deeper and inhaled the woodsy sent. Her eyes flew open. Dylan was asleep beside her. Her racing heart and alarm quickly calmed. She smiled as she slid from the bed, quietly grabbed her clothes and headed for the shower.

After her quick shower, she got dressed and eased the bedroom door shut behind her. She was spending her first Christmas with Dylan, and if the legend ended up being true, it wouldn't be her last. In her heart of hearts, she wanted the legend to be true. Stranger things had happened. Hell, her family was the textbook of strange. It was possible that he was meant to be included in the family tree.

Lily pushed all thoughts of the future away and concentrated on the here and now. She started picking up the mess they'd made from movie night on the floor. A memory she'd keep forever. She picked up the quilt and smiled as she admired the design. Boxes of different sizes and shapes, in greens and browns, had been sewn together with one patch of red sitting inside a box that didn't match the rest of the quilt. The better look she got of the quilt, the more the design took shape.

Lily folded it and placed it over the edge of the rocking chair. She paused, turning in place. Her gaze scanned the room and the stairs. The house was unusually quiet for the list of occupants that liked to visit.

She walked into the kitchen and started breakfast, hoping to surprise Dylan with pancakes in bed.

"Welcome to the family," a female voice said from beneath the archway.

Lily jumped at the voice, spinning around with a frying pan in her hand. She came face to face with a woman she'd never met in person but had seen in pictures.

"You're Dylan's mom."

The apparition floated into the room. "Maggie, but you can call me Mom."

"Don't you think that's putting the cart before the horse? We're still getting to know each other and just decided to start dating, if you want to call it that."

Maggie's smile was warm and inviting like Lily always imagined her mother-in-law's smile would be. Her hair fell down to her shoulders in soft waves of brown.

"I'm not worried. Your souls recognize each other as the twin flame."

"The twin what?"

"Soul mates, dear." Maggie moved around the kitchen and toward the back door. She stood for a moment looking outside. "You realize the size or value of the ruby doesn't matter. The magic of the Heart is the only thing that does." She turned slowly around. "Can you see it in your mind?" She gestured outside. "It's not out there."

Lily tilted her head. "No? Then do you care to tell me where I might find it?"

Maggie chuckled as she moved back into the room. "It's a puzzle for you and Dylan to solve together. It will take both of you to connect the pieces."

"Not even a hint?" Lily asked as she went back to making the pancakes.

"Not even a hint," Maggie answered. "But I am going to help you with your other problem."

Lily glanced over her shoulder. "And what's that?"

Maggie grinned. "Let's just say, the family you're going to marry into is a territorial bunch. You won't need to take the fight to them. When they show up tonight, we'll be waiting to help you."

"They wouldn't dare." Lily's eyes narrowed.

"I'm afraid they're already planning it. We may be dead, but we can still understand the living. Just wait until we start communicating with them." Maggie winked. "Why isn't Dylan cooking breakfast for you?"

"He's sleeping."

Maggie nodded and floated to the other side of the room. "Did he tell you where he made his fortune? It wasn't from his military wages."

She'd been bombarded with secrets the day he'd told her that he was rich. She hadn't even thought to ask. "Come to think of it....he didn't."

Maggie moved over to the counter. Her hand disappeared into the cabinet, and when she pulled it out, she had a bottle of cinnamon in her hand. She unscrewed the lid and shook some of the spices into the batter.

"You can manipulate objects?"

"Everyone in my family can, dear." She grinned as she reached into the sugar container and sprinkled a pinch of sugar into the batter. "Well, the dead one's anyway," she clarified.

Lily started mixing the batter. "Good to know."

"Merry Christmas, Lily," Maggie said as she dissipated from the room.

"Was that..." Dylan asked as he entered the room.

"If you were going to say your mother, you'd be right." Lily grinned and turned back around to pour the batter into the pan for the first batch of pancakes.

Dylan placed a kiss on Lily's lips and started a pot of coffee. "What did she have to say?"

"She told me to call her Mom." Lily grinned as she glanced over at Dylan.

"Tell me she didn't." Dylan's cheeks turned a cute tint of red.

"That and more." Lily tested the pancakes and flipped them. "Those men are coming for us tonight."

"Did she tell you that too?"

"Sure did." Lily grabbed a plate to put the pancakes on and took the cup of coffee that Dylan had poured her. "And that's not all. The ruby isn't in the mine."

"Really?" Dylan asked while sitting down at the table. He turned the chair to face her and stretched out his legs in front of him. "Did she bother to tell you where?"

"Nope." Lily put the pancakes on the plate before setting it in front of him. She leaned down and kissed his lips. "Merry Christmas."

"Merry Christmas, Lily."

Lily returned to the pan and started some more pancakes. "She also wanted to know why you weren't cooking and asked if I knew how you became a millionaire."

"Well, that's an easy one to answer. I told you about Rosa and cooking in her kitchen?"

"Yeah."

Dylan walked over to the cupboard and pulled down a jar of Alfredo sauce and put it in the middle of the table. "This is how."

Lily tilted her head, unsure what he meant. "I don't follow."

Dylan gestured to the jar. "This is mine. Well, mine and Rosa's. She let me concoct it in her kitchen, and she marketed it."

Lily's mouth parted. The sauce had been a staple in her kitchen for as long as Lily had known how to cook. "You're kidding."

He shook his head and took a bite of his pancake. He licked his lips. "Cinnamon and sugar."

"Compliments of your mother." Lily nodded and picked up the sauce and turned it to read the label. She scanned the contents and paused when she got to the manufacturer's name.

"That explains why they remind me of my childhood." Dylan chuckled.

"Sawyer Foods." She glanced up. "That's you and Rosa?"

He grinned. "Yep." He gestured to her plate. "You should eat before your pancakes get cold."

Lily took a bite of her pancakes. Dylan confused her, excited her and surprised her. Every day was a new emotion, making her feel alive as she lived in the moment.

****

Dylan loaded the last plate in the dishwasher. "What do you want to do today?"

She glanced at him, a smile on her face as she tossed the towel she'd used to dry her hands onto the counter. "When I was little, I wasn't your typical little girl. I don't think any of the Bennetts were except maybe Aunt Claire. Growing up with family members that were cops and working in security really changes the way a person thinks. We don't brag over the size of our cars and houses. We pull out our guns and show them off. It's just the way we grew up."

"Okay....are you telling me you want a gun for Christmas?"

She chuckled and walked to the back door. "I don't like the idea of those men on my property."

"If they get caught, they'll be arrested. I don't think they'd be that stupid."

"True."

He could see the wheels spinning, but he lacked the ability to read her decision.

"So, we beat them to the punch." She grinned. "They want to dig in the mine, we'll let them."

Dylan turned her in his arms. "But I thought..."

"They're looking for something they won't find. We both know there is an apparition in there trying to scare everyone out. How about we let the ghost have a go at the guys? What's the worst that can happen? They run scared? They leave empty-handed?"

"What about your Aunt Lydia?"

She grinned as she leaned in to kiss him. "We'll keep her on standby." She kissed him again. "You care to take a drive out to the lake with me?"

"I wouldn't let you go out there alone." And that was the truth. He wouldn't let her go alone, even if he had to hide in the shadows. The men she was going to meet were a shady bunch.

"Perfect. Let me grab my keys." She left him standing in the kitchen.

"She's taking a big gamble," his grandfather said from a corner in the kitchen.

"I agree," he answered and turned to face the man who had helped raise him. "You'll make sure they don't do much damage?"

"Of course," he answered, and with the blink of an eye, his grandfather was standing in front of him. "Tell her how you feel."

"I'm not going to scare her off. She's not ready yet, but I'll tell her when the time is right. I promise, old man."

"See that you do, kid. I'm betting your relationship is going to be the biggest and most satisfying adventure you'll ever have."

Dylan grinned. "I'm looking forward to it."

"Are you two going to gab like girls all day?" Lily asked from the archway.

Dylan chuckled and followed behind her out of the house. He should have been embarrassed, should have played it off, but there was no sense hiding his feelings. Not when he already knew he loved her. "How much of that did you hear?"

"Not much." Lily shrugged and slid behind the wheel of the SUV. "So what type of adventure are we going to have?" she asked before she gave a full-belly laugh.

"Loving you is going to be an adventure of a lifetime."

She quit laughing and turned to him. He fought to hide the smile from his lips.

"Loving me? You can't possibly love me. We just met."

He chuckled. "I've loved you since I was eight years old and the first time I heard the legend of the call."

"And yet you married?" she countered.

He shrugged. "How was I supposed to know the call was real and you actually existed?"

"Not to mention that you answered and didn't let it go to voicemail." She put the SUV into drive and started to drive toward the lake.

"Miracles do happen," he answered as he checked the items in his backpack. He wouldn't be caught in the presence of assholes without a way to protect her and himself. "Are you carrying?"

She reached into the glove box and pulled out a loaded holster. "I am now."

****

Lily eased down the path at the lake house. Hunters in bright orange were in the woods. Bear had been their choice of hunt for years on the adjacent property around the lake. The locals were vigilant about keeping the animals away from the lake homes.

Several trucks were parked outside, and a light shown through the window. Two guys were sitting in rockers on the porch with shotguns across their lap.

They rose as Lily pulled up in front of the cabin. They raised their guns, with fingers on the trigger but didn't make a move from the porch.

"Put on your holster," he ordered.

Lily slid the thigh holster on with the gun inside. There wouldn't be any hiding the fact that she was armed, and he wanted it that way. He slid his in the waistband of his jeans.

"Stay close," she whispered as she exited the SUV.

"Damn it," he cursed and was quick to follow her out.

"I'm looking for Mr. Sims."

One of the men lifted the gun. "Hold it right there, honey."

The other disappeared into the house and returned, following Mr. Sims. The man was dressed in a suit similar to the one he'd worn the other day.

"Ms. Bennett, well, this is a surprise."

"Kind of like the surprise you were planning for my house later tonight, Mr. Sims?" Lily smiled. *Yeah, I know the score, you bastard.*

The man was smart enough not to answer. The men on the porch each shared a look. "What can I do for you?"

"It's not what you can do for me, but what I can do for you. Consider it your Christmas present."

"Oh?" he questioned as he stepped down off the porch. He motioned for the men to lower their guns. "And just what can you do for me?"

"Give you access to my mine." She glanced at Dylan before turning back to the man. "Granted, there are rocks in the way from you trying to get in from another point, but seeing that today is a day of miracles, I'm granting you access to my property, but I have conditions."

Mr. Sims tilted his head. It was obvious she'd gotten his attention, even more obvious that he was skeptical. "What are your terms?"

"No guns." She raised her brow. "The first sign of guns and you're out. Not only are you out, but I'll file a restraining order against you and your associates, and I'll go after your company in a civil suit." She stepped forward. "And believe me, I'll win."

He gave a slow nod. "Fine."

Dylan moved to her side. "Including the snipers on the mountain. Not only are they not allowed on the property, we don't want them in town. So send their asses on their way."

"Now, son, what makes you think there were snipers on the hill?"

Dylan grinned and pointed to the two men standing right outside the door. "The day you trespassed, I saw them through my scope." His jaw ticked. "Both of them. They might have been watching her, but I was watching them, and you. They're gone. That's non-negotiable."

He glanced behind him and gave a slight nod. "Fine. What else?"

"It's going to be triple what the contract was, payable upfront to the Southall Children's Home, and that's before you step a foot on my ground and regardless of what you find or what you don't find."

"Now...wait a minute. I offered twice the amount."

"Then I guess you don't want access."

"Ms. Bennett, you drive a hard bargain."

"If you think that's hard, then you're going to love my next demand."

Mr. Sims pressed his thin lips together, his beady eyes narrowed. "What's that?"

"You have one week, and then you leave town, if you last that long. You do know the mine is haunted, right?"

"Now wait just a minute. I'm not afraid of ghosts, but one week? That's not enough time."

Lily shook her head. She wouldn't budge on the last demand. "Take it or leave it. You want in my mine, those are my demands." She stepped closer to the man who had planned to attack her home or worse. "You're lucky, really. I'd had plans for you and your men when you showed up tonight."

"You couldn't have..."

"Known? Of course I could. This is my town, and I know it like the back of my hand. You may think you have the upper hand, but you don't. So that's my offer, take it, leave it, or take your chances on my property. You have until tomorrow to decide and talk to whomever you report to. If you agree, you'll sign a contract agreeing to my stipulations, and then you can start the next day. My attorney will be in touch."

She turned, walked back to the SUV, and opened the door. "Or....you can take your chances and follow through on your plan, and I can guarantee you'll be limping as you retreat. That is if you live through the night. I hear the bears in the area get kind of territorial."

Dylan stepped slowly backward to the SUV, not willing to take his eyes off the men. He made a gesture from his eyes to theirs and back.

He slid into the SUV and closed the door. "You're just full of surprises and way too generous."

"It's either that or spend the night in the woods picking them off one by one." She turned to him and grinned. "And the law kind of frowns on civilians playing war games." She reversed down the drive and continued back out the way she'd entered. She grabbed her phone and called her lawyer, explained the situation, and apologized for the urgency of her request and the intrusion of talking to her during the holidays. Having been the family's attorney for over two decades, he's had several unusual requests. This was simple compared to most, and he didn't bat an eye about her demands.

"Well, I guess there's no need for your aunt tonight."

"At least for the night." She grinned. "It's going to be chaos at Aunt Claire's tonight. Are you ready for that?"

"I think I can handle it."

"We'll see about that." Lily chuckled.

13 CHAPTER

Lily and Dylan had a relaxing afternoon after finding the plans that John and her family wanted to look over. To her and Dylan's surprise, the property lines did include the entire mountain within its boundaries, a fact of which Dylan himself wasn't even aware. They'd both never bothered to look if the entire mountain was included within the lines. He'd teased and joked that maybe they could learn to prospect for other jewels as a hobby in their spare time. For the years he'd lived there, as far as he knew, not many people had been up on the mountainside.

Lily slowed to a stop in front of a gated fence and smiled at the man standing guard with a gun.

"Are we going to dinner on a military compound?" Dylan asked as he turned in his seat and watched the gate close behind them.

"This place is....special. My Aunt Claire owns the house, but it's on the same property as Tactical Maneuvers, my father's company." She gave him a sideways glance as he turned back around. "I guess you could say that my family attracts trouble."

Dylan unbuckled as Lily parked and then stepped out. He grabbed the plans from the backseat and carried them beneath his arm. The house was decorated with streaming lights and wreaths. Garland stretched the length of the porch railing, and candles were lit in each window.

"I feel bad that I didn't bring presents," she murmured beneath her breath.

"I'm sure they understand," Dylan offered. "After everything you've been through."

The front door to Claire's house flew open, and Butch and Aunt Claire greeted them with warm and inviting smiles. Uncle Butch was dressed in his typical jeans and T-shirt while Aunt Claire had on a festive red sweater and slacks. Her definition of casual was never the same as the rest of the family. "Uncle Butch, Aunt Claire, you know Dylan."

"Of course." Aunt Claire smiled. "We're glad you decided to come. Please come in."

Aunt Claire ushered them inside. Soft Christmas music played through the house. The fireplace was lit with a small fire, the tree lights were on, and presents were overflowing beneath it. John's wife, Delaney, was trying as she might to keep the kids out of the presents. Platters of cookies sat near where they had set up a board game.

"The others are in the kitchen," Butch said as he led the way, walking next to Dylan.

Claire linked her arm with Lily's and leaned in to whisper in her ear. "How are things going with you two?"

Aunt Claire wasn't one to beat around the bush, and why should she when all she had to do was pick people's brains to find the answers? Her gift had come in handy in the past when bad guys wouldn't talk or when the younger Bennetts were hiding information. She would always be called in to use her gift. One glimpse of her headed in Lily's direction and Lily would be singing like a canary. There was no point in trying to hide the truth, not when any of the Bennetts were around, but especially her.

"Things are good. It's still new, and with all of the stuff going on at the property, we've still managed to enjoy each other's company."

Claire patted Lily's arm. "I'm glad."

They all walked into the kitchen where the rest of the family was congregating. Lily loved this kitchen and the use of the space. It was huge. There was a long island with pots and pans hanging overhead. All of the appliances were stainless steel set against granite countertops. Off of the kitchen was a long breakfast table that, if Lily had to guess, was used when the formal dining room wasn't called for. Her mom and aunts, Abby, Elizabeth, and Lydia, were in the kitchen cooking and chatting while they sipped glasses of wine.

Lily's dad and uncles, Mike, Ryan, and Rick, were sitting at the table, each with a beer in front of them while John had his head poked in the fridge. He pulled out two beers and offered one to Dylan.

"Lily," her mom squealed and hurried over pulling her into a hug. She tucked a strand of hair behind Lily's ear. "Everything okay?"

"So far." Lily grinned.

"Glad you could make it, squirt. Are those the property plans?" John asked.

"Yep. We took a look, and we're both a little shocked that it included the entire mountain." Dylan handed John the plans.

"Great." He unrolled the plans, which showed the property line, out on the table.

"About that..." Lily headed over to the table. "I made a deal with Sims."

Mike was taking a swig of beer and almost choked at her statement. He covered his mouth. "You made a deal with that asshole?"

"Language, dear," Elizabeth called from the other room, and Lily grinned.

"With stipulations of course," she amended as the rest of the women in the kitchen came to stand around the table. Lily could feel the unease in the room. Their concerned looks were evident as they all were probably silently questioning whether Lily had lost her mind.

Dylan moved to stand next to Lily, slipping his fingers through hers in a silent show of support.

"He can mine, but only for one week. He has to donate the sixty thousand dollars he was going to pay me to the children's home, and after his week is over, if they don't leave before then because they got scared, he has to leave town." Lily bit her lip waiting for the yelling to commence. Her aunts and uncles wouldn't like the idea; she'd known it going in.

"Lily...." Uncle Mike started to say.

Dylan jumped in to set her uncle at ease. "No guns. The first sign of firearms and they're off the property with a lawsuit and restraining order to keep them away."

"Are you getting this in writing?" her dad asked.

"Of course," she answered.

Uncle Butch crossed his arms over his chest. "I don't like it." His face was set in a scowl. "Even if they do sign a contract, who's to say they're going to follow the guidelines?" He turned to Lily's dad. "We'll set up a team to monitor them. It's just for a week."

"Oh, Uncle Butch, I couldn't ask you to do that."

"Of course you can," Dylan answered. He rested his palm on Lily's arms. "Be smart, Lily. They were going to ambush your property tonight. I could use the extra firepower."

"What!" Emma barked. "Oh no, they weren't." She turned to Aunt Abby. "Where's your gun? They aren't touching my baby."

Lily's dad rose from the chair and circled his arms around her mom. "Calm down, honey. Nothing is going to happy to Lily. I promise."

"You're damn right," Emma responded. "Lily, you're coming home with me."

Lily fought against rolling her eyes. Her mother meant well, even if it was a bit of overkill. "Mom, everything will be okay."

"Of course it will," John added. "Especially since Tactical will be onsite monitoring their progress. We'll set up a couple sharpshooters in the woods, guards in and out, and we'll wire the whole damn place if we have to. Nothing will touch her, not with me and Dylan there."

Claire moved closer to Butch. "Why would you let them on your property if they were going to attack you tonight? I don't understand your reasoning."

Lily stepped over to the coffee pot and poured herself a cup. "That's easy. They were coming with or without my permission. Dylan's dad signed a contract, and this will keep me out of court and the children will be getting a good sum of money just for letting the jerks step foot on my property." She took a sip. "Besides, I think they'll run scared before they get very far. I have it on good authority that the mine is haunted, or well...if it's not already, then it will be." Lily grinned.

"As grown up and rational as that all sounds, I still don't like it," Uncle Ryan, the ex-FBI agent, announced.

"Neither do I," Claire chimed in. She threaded her arm around her husband's. "Butch, honey, you need to send a team to watch her woods tonight, just in case."

"I can't ask you to send your men on Christmas. They have families," Lily argued.

"We'll ask for volunteers and make it worth their time," Claire answered.

Aunt Abby threaded her arm through Lily's and pulled her away from the group. "You still have the guns I gave you last Christmas?"

"Of course," Lily answered.

"Good. Just remember everything I taught you. You don't walk outside without one. You stay alert to anything out of the ordinary; you call for backup before you jump in headfirst. I know that last one is a bit of stretch, but I'd hate to have to kill that guy."

"I'm going to be fine, Aunt Abby."

"Of course she is," John added while tossing his arm around her shoulder. "She's got me."

"And Dylan," Lily added, walking away from the duo. She linked her fingers through his. "He also has military training and knows the property like the back of his hand."

"You need a job, kid?" Butch asked.

Dylan chuckled. "Not yet, but thanks for asking."

Planning consumed a majority of the evening. Phone calls were made, and texts were being sent. When her family went into action mode, there was no bringing them back out of it until Lily's mom and aunts had enough and rounded the room collecting cell phones and computers.

The meal was one of the best that Lily had had in a long time. It wasn't necessarily the food but the company. She'd missed her family, all of them. After the children opened the presents and the room was cleaned, Lily and Dylan said their goodbyes, with much protest from Lily's mom, who was still arguing that Lily should spend the night in her childhood home.

****

Dylan should have known a quick escape wasn't possible with this highly in-tune and gifted bunch. It had taken them an hour just to get through the door and to the SUV. When he noticed Lily's Aunt Lydia, the visionary of the bunch, sneak outside, slowly closing the door behind her, her actions should have told him something was wrong. Lydia stepped over to Dylan's side of the SUV as he tossed the property plans into the back seat. He shut the door and grabbed the handle on the passenger side, ready to climb in. Lydia stopped him.

"Dylan, I don't know what the family has told you about me, but sometimes I get visions, and I had one about you and Lily. I don't know how to tell you this."

"Just tell me," he answered as he held his breath preparing for the worse.

"In order for her to live, you're going to have to let her go."

"I don't understand."

"I can't tell you more. All I can tell you is that it will be one the hardest decisions you'll ever make."

Dylan shook his head and crossed his arms over his chest. "I'll never let her go."

Lydia touched his arm. "If you love her, then have faith in her and let her go. It's the only way."

Lydia gave a quick squeeze to Dylan's arm before hurrying back into the house.

Dylan climbed in the SUV.

"What was that about?" Lily asked.

Dylan's mind raced with Lydia's words and what they implied. *If you love her let her go.* Did that mean they were going to have problems? What the hell was that supposed to mean? Did she mean it literally? The woman had talked in riddles about something that wouldn't happen. There was no way he'd do anything to run Lily off. He'd just found her.

"She had a vision that I was supposed to let you go."

"What!" Lily's gaze shot to the closed door. She was about to get out of the vehicle before he stopped her.

"She must be mistaken, Lily. I just found you."

Lily's collapsed back into the leather seat, looking at the front door.

"Let me just be clear. I'm not letting you go, unless you tell me to take a hike."

Lily grinned. "Then I guess we don't have a problem." She turned the SUV around in the drive and started heading toward the gate.

They waited for the gate to slide open, and then she turned to him again, a look of certainty in her eyes. "I'm not ready to let you go either."

Dylan leaned over into her seat and cupped her cheek. He pressed his lips to hers in a kiss he'd been dying to give her all night. "Then we're in agreement."

"Yes."

They drove back to Lily's in a comfortable silence. He wasn't sure if it was the fact that they were both on the same page or if she'd been thinking about what her aunt had said. Either way, they were together and in agreement. He wasn't letting her go, and she wasn't asking. The rest of the evening should have been one of ease and relaxation, but later, he'd slipped from the bed and pulled up a chair by the window, his rifle lying across his lap. Unease settled in his spine and a foreboding pressure pressed against his head, forming the first headache he'd had in a long time.

She might believe that her offer to Sims would thwart his plans, but Dylan was taking up point in the event she was wrong. He slipped downstairs and grabbed the quilt from the rocking chair and used it to cover his legs and get comfortable by the window in her room. It was the highest vantage point they had. He glanced over to Lily.

"Nothing is going to happen to you. I swear it," he whispered into the silent room before resuming his watch.

14 CHAPTER

Dylan sipped the last of his coffee in an attempt to stay alert. After hours of sitting in the chair, his eyes had turned glassy, and he had a hard time keeping his lids open. The house was quiet, too quiet. He stood, raising his hands over his head and leaned backward and to each side, stretching his back before heading downstairs to start another pot. He waited patiently before he took his first sip of the warm liquid in hopes that it would keep him awake as he stared out the back door. His eyes scanned the area, watching for anything more than a leaf being blown across the yard. A spotlight on the side of the house flickered before it went off. A blown bulb, perhaps, but he wasn't going to risk it. Movement in the shadows caught his eye, and his heart raced. A silhouette dressed in black was quick to disappear.

"Like hell." Dylan checked the lock on the back door and hurried through the house and out the front. He eased off the porch, his gun clutched in his hand. He quietly rounded the side of the house, his back pressed against the brick as he tiptoed toward where the light had gone out.

He'd done this several times before when he'd snuck out of the house. He knew there was a water spigot around the corner. He knew that there was a bush he'd have to step around, and at the back of the house, a garden where he'd leave a footprint behind if he wasn't careful. He stopped at the edge of the house and peered around the corner toward the pool. The light at the other corner of the house had been shut off, and someone was at the back door, kneeling down, trying to jimmy the lock.

Dylan stepped out, his gun raised at the man with a black ski mask covering his face. He stepped carefully forward as he looked down the barrel of his gun.

"Drop it." Lily's voice came from the other corner of the house. Her silhouette, just an outline in the darkness with a gun in hand, stepped forward toward the figure. "One wrong move and you aren't walking out of here."

Dylan moved on silent feet, approaching the man from behind.

Lily spotted him, and her gun lowered only slightly.

"Put your hands on your head," Lily demanded.

The criminal was slow to comply.

Dylan stuffed his gun in his jeans, came up from behind, and grabbed the man around the neck. He ripped the mask off his head and watched in shock as Lily lowered her gun and raised her hand to her chest.

"I almost killed you," she said, shaking her head. "What are you doing here?"

Dylan whipped the man around to get a better look at the intruder's face. John grinned. "I just finished checking the property and wanted to see if you'd hear or see me coming."

"A test?" Dylan asked as he let John go.

"Of course." John grinned. "You guys are on your game tonight." He patted Dylan on his back. "I brought a few other guys with me. We'll take the watch for the rest of the night.

"Get some rest, Lily Bug. Sims has already contacted the lawyer and has agreed to the contract."

"Wait....how do you know that?"

John grinned. "I have my ways." He wiggled his brows before jogging back into the darkness and disappearing out of sight.

****

Lily and Dylan walked back into the house and locked up before they made their way back to bed. This time he didn't fight the urge to close his eyes. He pulled her close, his gun within reach, and held on to the woman he was going to spend the rest of his life with. For now she was safe, but for seven days straight, he'd be hard-pressed to close his eyes, not when Sims, his snipers, and band of merry bandits might be nearby.

The next morning, Dylan jogged down the stairs to find Lily cooking breakfast for a group of men that Dylan had never met. She introduced them all as her father's employees, yet they bantered with her like they'd known her all of her life. She was as comfortable with them as she was with the guns they were carrying. It was evident she'd lived this life and been through similar situations. She was strong, so much stronger than he'd ever given her credit for. Not once had she broken down or acted weak.

****

Lily served Dylan the last batch of pancakes with a kiss on his cheek. The poor guy was in a house full of strangers and yet took everything in stride. Lily had grabbed the plans from the car and brought them into the house for John and the others to review. He'd opened them and had the drawings spread out, Dylan by his side, as they talked in hushed tones and made plans to have men stationed throughout the woods. Lily stood at the end of the table, looking at the plans from a side angle. Her gaze travelled around the blocks indicating the rooms in the house. She'd seen that design before, but where she hadn't a clue. It wasn't the same looking at the rooms from straight on, but it was similar when viewed long ways, from the side. She was sure she'd seen that design before.

She pushed the thoughts from her mind and announced she was going to get a shower. She told them that she'd cook them all dinner later, and for whoever else was on duty working the entrance, as Sims and his men came in with their heavy equipment to move the fallen boulders out of the way. He'd actually taken her seriously that he had only a week. Trying to move those big rocks by hand would have eaten up much of that time.

Dylan walked into the room as she was gathering things for her shower. He pulled her into his arms and kissed her lips. "Lily, there's something I have to tell you."

"What's that?" she asked as she relaxed in his embrace.

"I love you. I'll love you until the day I die."

"That sounds like the Ruby talking."

He shook his head. "That's my heart talking." He kissed her once more and released her, turning to leave.

"Dylan..."

He stopped at the door and winked. "I'm going down to the mine to help the others keep a close eye on Sims and his guys. Do me a favor and stay in the house."

She grinned. "I'll try."

Lily took her time in the shower, letting the warm spray of the water ease her tense muscles. Dylan loved her. Butterflies took flight in her stomach. Did she love him? Was it too soon, too quick since they'd met? Was it an effect of the missing Ruby? She had to find it. There was only one way to make sure he wasn't under a spell, only one way she'd ever know the truth and not question whether he was giving his heart to her freely. "I have to find it."

"Then find it you will," she heard Maggie say.

Lily whipped back the curtain while using it to cover her body. "Hello?" she called out to the empty room. No one answered.

She got out of the shower, dressed, and was latching her watch on her wrist as she walked into her bedroom. The quilt was spread out sideways on the bed. Her gun was sitting inside the red box. The house plans were spread out above it.

She glanced around the room, hoping to see who had left it out. Lily picked up the gun and stuffed it in the back of her jeans, pulling her shirt over top of it. She studied the quilt in detail. Three rows of boxes, it looked like the house plans. She ran her finger over the boxes, calling out the rooms by name. Her finger landed on the last one, the red one at the bottom and closest to her.

"I'll be a son of a bitch. Walter did find the damn thing and hid it...." She ran her finger over the entire box before touching just over the single strip of red. "In the basement. It couldn't possibly....could it have been that easy? No..." She warred with herself.

She took a picture of the box with her phone to compare the red in the box to the actual layout. She jogged down to the first floor. The house was quiet as she made her way down the hall and to the basement entrance.

She opened the door and eased down the old wooden stairs. She pulled the string hanging in her way to turn on the light before she reached the last stair.

The musky smell of the basement reminded her of an older person's home. The place needed to be aired out. Her gaze went to the small windows, and she silently wondered how long it had been since they'd been opened.

Lily pulled out her phone and brought up the picture. She stood at the stairs and compared it to her vantage point at the end of the stairs. She shook her head. From where she was standing, she couldn't see the whole room. She moved farther inside and repositioned until she could see the whole space and her gaze wasn't blocked by the wall that ran the length of the stairs.

The red fabric was on the right in the box, in the corner to be exact. She glanced in that direction shocked to find the hot water heater where the red in the box was located. She shoved her phone back in her pocket and walked closer to the heater. She pressed her head against the wall, trying to look behind it and circled it, pressing her head against the other wall for a better view. Nothing. Well nothing that she could tell.

Lily turned the knobs of the water off, knowing that it might be a long time before she got a warm shower again. She shrugged and unhooked the valves. Using all of her might, she walked the hot water heater by rolling it out of her way to get a better look at the area behind it. There was a three-by-three area that didn't match the rest of the bricks.

She eased down onto her knees and tried to move the bricks with her hands. They didn't budge. She glanced behind her and spotted a hammer and a shovel. She pushed to her feet and grabbed them both, along with a crow bar, hoping that one might do the trick.

She started with the shovel, and it was awkward and not easy to manipulate in the small area, so she ditched it and tossed it behind her. She picked up the hammer and the crow bar. She held the crow bar against the very old mortar holding the bricks in place. She hit the bar with the hammer and slowly chipped her way around the first brick. Using the crowbar, she eased the brick from its spot and continued to work on the rest. After the third brick, she peered inside, using the backlight of her phone to illuminate the small space.

Her breath caught in her throat as the light bounced off the clearest, biggest, red ruby she'd ever seen. A tear of joy trickled down her cheek as excitement built in her chest. She reached inside and eased the priceless gem out, her heart beating wildly that she'd solved the mystery. Her hands shook with the realization that the story was real and she'd found what others had not.

"I have to tell Dylan."

"You know how you told me I could play in your room?" Mel said, appearing beside her.

"Yeah."

"There's a mean man that was in the living room, and he's coming down the stairs."

"Stand up nice and slow," Sims said from behind her.

Lily glanced over her shoulder, and her mouth parted. The man to whom she'd given permission to search the mine was standing behind her, holding a gun pointed at her head.

Lily eased to her feet at the same moment Melanie vanished out of sight.

Sims glanced down at the stone in her hand, and his thin lips split into a grin. "I knew the minute you gave me access to the mine that we wouldn't find it there." He walked farther into the room with the gun trained at her chest. "We're leaving, nice and slow, and I won't kill you."

"You aren't going to get away with this."

"Sure I am, you twit." The word made Lily's blood boil. She clutched the Ruby tighter in her hand, silently wondering if she knocked him over the head with the gem if it might knock him out. "You're my ticket out of here."

Lily's cell phone rang, and she didn't have to look at the caller ID to know who it was. Her mother would be bent over in cramps at the first mention of trouble. Her mom would know, and worse, she might come to try to stop Sims and get herself killed.

"I have to answer that," she whispered to Sims.

"No, you don't."

"You don't understand. It's my mother. If I don't answer it, then she'll be here in less than five minutes. I have to answer it."

The phone stopped ringing for a quick heartbeat before it started again.

Sims stepped closer to her and held the gun to her head. "No tricks."

Lily pulled the phone out of her pocket. "Hey, Mom."

"What kind of pie do you want for dinner? Chocolate, pecan, lemon or broccoli?"

At the mention of the word broccoli, Lily knew exactly what her mother was asking. She wanted to know Lily's status. She was using the codes words that had been instilled in her since childhood. Chocolate, the easiest for all of her aunts to remember because it was a favorite, meant they couldn't speak freely, but they were fine. Pecans were used to tell the others they were fine but should probably stay away from the house. Lemons meant trouble, the call-the-police kind of trouble and get them here quick. The last code word was the most severe. If the words were ever muttered, everyone scattered to a prearranged destination, having no contact until they'd all met up together. They hadn't had to use the last one yet but had instituted it just in case, for emergencies.

There wasn't a chance in hell any of their family members would be confused by this request. They'd came up with a code word that was avoided like the plague but still subtle enough not to attract the kind of attention that one of them screaming, "run for your life," would bring. *Broccoli*. There wasn't a member of their family that could stomach the green veggie.

"Lemon pie for dinner sounds great."

The line went quiet. "Lemon pie. Got it."

Lily hung up the phone and went to shove it back in her pocket.

"Oh no, you don't. I'll take that." Sims slid the phone from her fingers, dropped it to the ground, and stepped on the piece, cracking the glass screen. With each pound of his boot, another piece fell off the phone.

15 CHAPTER

Dylan and John stood at the tree line watching as equipment was brought in to move the big boulders. Trucks entered behind it, and workers started to pile out.

"They didn't waste any time."

"They sure didn't." Dylan scratched his chin. "I can't believe my dad signed a contract with Sims. It's out of character."

John shrugged. "Maybe he was thinking that the guy wouldn't find anything."

"I'm sure you're right," Dylan answered. "Can I see your binoculars?"

"Sure." John lifted the strap over his head and handed them over to Dylan.

"What do you see?" John asked.

"It's what I don't see," Dylan answered as he pressed his eyes against the holes to get a better look and scanned the area. "For a man who was so gung-ho about mining, you would think that he would be here to supervise the efforts."

"You're right," John answered, pulling the radio from his belt.

"Gunther, what's your status?"

They were met with static instead of a reply.

"Who's Gunther?"

"The man I left guarding Lily's front door," John answered. "Status check, Gunther."

The line clicked on twice, but no voice came out.

John picked up the phone and called the office. "I need a perimeter check and security sweep of the cameras at Lily's house. Gunther isn't calling in his status."

John paced a well-worn path and abruptly stopped. "What!"

Melanie appeared by Dylan's side. John continued with his conversation as Dylan dropped down to his knees. "What's wrong?"

"There's a bad man."

"With Lily?"

"I like her. Don't let the bad man hurt her." Mel disappeared.

"Shit." Dylan knocked John on the shoulder. "We need to go. We need to go now. Lily's in trouble."

John hit End on the phone. "Sims and another guy are in her house. They tied Gunther up, and they have her at gunpoint."

Dylan jumped into the passenger side of John's truck and prayed the entire way that he wasn't too late. John took the corner doing forty and barely swerved to miss one of the trees. He pulled into the driveway, kicking up dust as he threw the vehicle into park, and they both jumped out.

Lily's front door opened, and Dylan's heart started beating again. He met Lily's scared gaze and then saw the big red ruby in her hand. "You found it."

"I knew she would," Sims announced, holding the gun to her head as he shoved her out of the door.

The tattooed man that Dylan had seen Sims talking to in town a few days ago was walking beside him. His gun was aimed at Dylan. "Don't even think about it."

"I'm not letting you leave with her," Dylan said as he gave a slow shake of his head. "It's not happening."

"Get out of my way, or she gets a bullet to the head."

A tear fell down Lily's face. "You have to let me go."

Dylan shook his head and lifted the gun higher. "No. You can have the ruby, but she stays."

"Dylan, don't do anything stupid," John said calmly and moved to stand beside Dylan.

Sims cocked the trigger. "Sorry, kid, but she's coming with me. She's my ticket out of this town."

"It's okay, Dylan. The family will find me, just like when I used to drink beer at the lake." She tried to reason with him. She used her pointer finger to tap on the wristband of her watch several times. "You have to let me go."

"Lily...."

She shook her head and tried to give him a reassuring smile. "I love you."

"Aw....how touching," Sims said as he jerked her arm and started pulling her toward the waiting van.

The man with the tattoo was walking backward, his gun pointed in their direction. Sims grinned as he jerked Lily to a halt. He aimed at John's SUV and pulled the trigger twice, taking out two of John's tires. Tattooed guy lifted his gun and shot in Dylan's direction.

Both Dylan and John dove to the ground to avoid the shot. Lily screamed, and Dylan watched in horror as Sims lifted the butt of his gun and knocked her in the side of the head. Her legs gave out and her body slumped to the ground. He set the ruby in the van before scooping Lily up and throwing her inside.

"That son of a bitch," Dylan growled and pulled his gun, aiming it at the tattooed man as he was climbing into the van. The bullet pierced the window and struck him in the shoulder.

John shot and took out his leg. The impact sent the man flying backward.

The van tires squealed, leaving the tattooed asshole behind as collateral damage. The driver swerved, forcing John and Dylan to jump out of the way.

Dylan got to his feet and stormed over to the man with the tattoo. He held him at gunpoint.

"John, you all right?"

"Yeah," he answered, walking up beside him with the phone on speaker. "Get those assholes off the property and start the trace on Lily's watch."

"Sir, it's already been called in," the man on the other end replied.

Dylan shared a glance with John. "By whom?"

"Emma Bennett. We started the trace twenty seconds ago. The family is on the way to her property. Their ETA is seven minutes."

"Which way is the tracker heading?"

"North."

"The airport," Dylan said through gritted teeth. "We can't let them get airborne."

"Reroute the Bennetts. Send them to the private airport out of town. If the tracker veers off course, text me immediately."

Dylan ran inside and grabbed his backpack and Lily's keys. He tossed John the keys to Lily's SUV. "You drive."

They hurried into the vehicle and did a donut in Lily's driveway. They couldn't have gotten too far. Right now they had the element of surprise. Sims wouldn't know that they knew where Sims was heading.

"We'll get her back," John said reassuringly.

"This asshole is mine," Dylan answered while glancing toward John. "You grab Lily and get her to safety. I'll take care of Sims."

John tossed Dylan his phone the second it beeped, letting him know he'd gotten a text.

"They veered off course and are heading toward the lake."

"Sims is going to the lake house," Dylan announced.

John grinned. "Sounds like the tides are starting to turn in our favor. We know those houses and woods better than anyone else in town." John glanced at Dylan. "If I know my cousin, and they don't have her hands bound, she isn't going to wait around to be rescued. She's going to give them one hell of a fight before she runs for it."

"She's going to get herself killed." Dylan balled his fist, taking a deep, long breath to try and calm his urge to hit something until he came face to face with Sims.

****

Lily blinked her eyes open in an unfamiliar place. She raised a hand to stop the pounding in her head. The metal of the van was pressed into her back as she slid to the wall while the driver took a corner.

Sims was sitting on a bench seat, his gun resting across his lap while he studied the ruby, lifting it to the light.

Lily closed her eyes, watching him from beneath her lashes. Her family would be on the way. After giving the code to her mom, and then making sure that Dylan and John remembered the tracker, the family would be on the way for sure. It was just a matter of stalling the assholes when they stopped.

She eyed the door mechanism, wondering if it was locked or if Sims had bothered. She formed a plan in her head.

There was no way this guy was leaving town with her, much less Dylan's ruby.

The van slowed to a stop. It was now or never. Lily eased the gun from the waistband of her jeans, making a mental note to thank Dylan's mother for placing it on the quilt.

Sims still sat in his seat with the ruby in his hand. The door mechanism unlatched, and the door slid open.

Lily lifted her gun and pulled the trigger hitting the man in the shoulder, making the man at the door fall to his knees. She snatched the ruby from Sims' hand and shoved his gun. It flew toward the front of the van. Within seconds, she'd jumped from the van, her gun in one hand and the ruby in the other. She hit the ground running, and quickly recognizing where she was, she held in her grin.

Her family owned a lake house not too far from where she was. If she could get there, she could barricade herself in, have access to more guns, and call in the cavalry, if they weren't already on their way.

"You stupid bitch," Sims yelled as a bullet whizzed by Lily's head.

Lily chanced a glance over her shoulder. Sims was running after her, his long legs eating up the distance between them. He raised the gun and fired again.

"Shit." She spun back around just in time to miss tripping over a fallen log. She wasn't going to make it to her house. He was too fast. Within seconds, he'd catch her if she didn't die running.

Her eyes scanned the horizon, searching for a good place to hide the Ruby. There wasn't one. He was too close, and there was no way she could shake him.

Her lungs burned the longer she ran with her breaths coming out in pants as she used a ballerina move to jump over a bear trap on the ground she wasn't sure was even legal to use in a hunt. She sailed over the metal, missing its steel clutches. *Thanks for the lessons, Mom.* She stopped suddenly in place, turning and training her gun on him. She stepped backward, drawing him near until she was standing next to a large tree. She dropped the Ruby behind the trunk. She lifted her gun and shot in Sims' direction.

He slowed to a walk, his breathing labored. "You missed, honey."

"That was a warning. Don't come any closer."

He grinned, his gun pointed in her direction. "Looks like we've got a stand-off because I'm not leaving these woods without that Ruby."

"Neither am I," she said through gritted teeth. "Standard revolver. You fired two into the tires and shot three times at me. You've got one bullet left, whereas I have a full clip."

"I only need one shot." He chuckled as he continued to walk slowly in her direction.

Lily's gaze went from Sims to the trap and back. Just a few more steps and it would be game over.

"You want it, come and take it from me in a fair fight." She took a gamble and lowered her gun.

"And here all this time I thought you were smart." He sneered as his foot hit the trap, setting the mechanism off. The jaws clamped around his leg, tearing into the skin. Sims screamed and fired his last bullet in her direction.

The bullet pierced her shoulder, the force sending her head back forcefully to smack into the tree. Her eyes rolled into the back of her head, and she collapsed to the ground.

****

Dylan's heart almost stopped beating when he found Lily unconscious on the ground. He slid to his knees next to her. He reached for her then paused, not knowing if he should touch her or not. Blood was oozing from her shoulder. He tore off his shirt and pressed it to her wound.

"Is she...?" John's worried tone indicated he wondered the same thing Dylan did.

He reached for her neck. Her pulse was slow, but he could feel it. "She's alive," he called back over his shoulder. "She needs an ambulance."

"Stay with me, Lily, please baby...stay with me." He tried to soothe her as he cupped her cheek, trying to rouse her with just his voice.

John had pulled out his phone and was barking orders to whomever he was calling when the rest of the Bennetts arrived. It took three of her uncles to pry Dylan away so that Lily's Aunt Elizabeth could get close enough to treat her. Sirens screamed in the distance, growing louder the closer the vehicles came.

John rounded the scene, trying to get a closer look at Lily. He picked up the ruby and held it out to Dylan. "Looks like she found your Heart."

Dylan took the ruby but kept his eyes on Elizabeth, inching closer so that he could be near Lily again.

16 CHAPTER

Lily turned her head from the offending smell. When it reached her nostrils for the second time, she turned in the other direction.

"She's coming around," her Aunt Elizabeth announced.

Lily blinked her eyes open, the pain in her shoulder gone. The commercial fluorescent lights in her view flickered. Her aunt was holding smelling salts under Lily's nose. "Where am I?"

"You're in the hospital, sweetie."

"Where's my mom?"

"I'm right here." Emma moved to her bedside and squeezed her hand.

"Joe died." Lily frowned, remembering while letting a tear slip down her face. "He left me alone." A concerned look passed between her mother and aunt.

"Lily. Do you know what day it is?"

She shook her head, and her brows dipped. Her brain hurt to think. She lifted a hand to her head to stop the pain. "It hurts to think."

"That's okay," Emma said while brushing back the hair on Lily's forehead. "Everything is going to be okay. You're safe."

The door to her hospital room opened, and a man that Lily had never seen before walked in carrying a bouquet of roses. Confused, she glanced at her mother and squeezed her hand.

"Lily."

Lily shook her head. "Do I know you?"

The man met Emma's gaze before meeting hers again. "I'm Dylan," he said as he stepped forward. "Don't you remember?"

"No," Lily whispered. "Have we met?"

He stepped closer. "Lily, you have to remember. I love you."

Lily squirmed back farther into the bed, hoping that it would swallow her up.

Lily's father took the man by the elbow. "I think we should let her rest." He guided the guy out of the room and into the hallway.

Elizabeth gave Lily a sad smile. "You hit your head pretty hard. We're going to run some tests."

"Can my mom stay?"

"Of course, sweetie."

****

Lily's father, Jake, escorted Dylan from the room and into the hall.

"Why doesn't she know me?" Dylan asked as he followed Jake down the hall toward the waiting room.

"Not only was she shot, but she hit her head. We won't know the extent of the damage until they run more tests." Jake poured them both some coffee and sat down in the one of the chairs.

"What does this mean? Is she ever going to remember? Did she forget everything?"

Jake placed his hand on Dylan's shoulder. "I'm not sure, but if you got her to fall in love with you once, you can do again."

An hour later, Elizabeth walked into the waiting room, hugging a clipboard against her chest. "Well, there's good news and bad news. Which do you want first?"

Jake answered for them both. "The bad."

"She has amnesia, which is obvious. Her recollection stops before she met Dylan." She tilted her head toward Jake. "She remembers walking you and Emma to the door on her first night in the house, and that's it."

Dylan's gut clenched, and his heart ached. "And the good news?"

"We don't think it's permanent," Elizabeth announced.

"How long until she remembers everything?" Dylan ran his hand through his hair.

"It could be an hour, a week, or months, but the memories should all return."

Dylan let out a breath he didn't realize he'd been holding. She would remember him, eventually. That was the best thing he'd heard yet.

"Can I see her?" Dylan asked.

Elizabeth shared a look with Jake. "Not today. We'd like to make sure she's stable when she's taken home and feels safe in her environment. We know you'd never do anything to hurt her, but you have to remember, she doesn't know who you are, and it might take some time."

Dylan gave a slow nod. "Tomorrow?"

"Emma is going to take her home and stay with her for the night to keep an eye on her. Do you have somewhere else you can stay?"

"He's staying with us," Claire announced as she entered the room. "It's my fault his apartment is being renovated, so he'll stay with us until it's done or she remembers. Whichever comes first."

"I couldn't possibly..."

Jake patted him on the back. "Just give in. She's going to get her way. The Bennett women always do."

****

Dylan called Emma and Jake daily in search of updates. He'd hoped Lily might remember him by the New Year's Eve party. He'd planned for it to be a night she'd never forget. His shoulders sagged in defeat as he was told, once again, that she didn't remember anything. He stood at the kitchen window looking out into Claire's garden as he hung up the phone.

"You look like shit," John announced as he walked up next to him.

"I miss her."

"I have faith she'll remember. She's one of the strongest people I know."

"It sucks I can't see her."

"Let's take a walk." John opened the back door, and they walked outside and followed a path toward the outcrop of trees. He stopped and turned to face Dylan. "My wife was stabbed right here, in this very spot. Granted, she wasn't my wife at the time, but she was pregnant with my daughter." He glanced down to the ground.

"My world crumbled. My heart stopped beating, and my life flashed before my eyes."

John looked up at Dylan. "I realized that day what matters most. It wasn't the perfect job or anything else. She mattered, she and my daughter."

Dylan glanced back down at the ground.

"When we Bennetts fall, we fall hard. There's normally some gunfire or knives slicing in the air, and in my case, an exploding house, but my point is, we experience the worst first, and if you two can beat that, then the rest is icing on the cake. The best is yet to come, and normally better because you'll have a deeper appreciation of what living really means."

John turned around and led the way back to the house. "She loves you. I know she does. And if you love her, then that's all that matters. The rest will work itself out, now that the guns and bad guys are out of the way. Now come on, you have to get ready for the big shindig. There's no way you're sitting this one out."

"Will she...."

"Yes," John answered. "I already stopped by and talked to her."

****

Lily held her glass of champagne and grinned as her family and Aunt Claire's guests milled around the room. The soft Christmas music was a melody to her ears. Garland was strung down the banisters and around the room. The twenty-foot Christmas tree was decorated to perfection in colors of gold and green. Laughter came from a nearby group of women, and a few smaller kids hurried by, each with cookies in their hands. This was the type of Christmas she remembered having, not the one she would have planned herself, but her family was there, and that mattered most.

Lily couldn't quit looking at the man across the room. Their eyes met, and she could feel the magnetic pull toward the man who had shown up in her hospital room. The same man she couldn't remember.

Her cousin stepped up beside her. "Do you remember him yet?"

Lily took another sip of her champagne. "I remember his face, but I can't remember his name or how I know him."

John rubbed her back. "It's okay, you will."

John went to walk off, but Lily grabbed his arm, stopping him. "What's his name?"

She had to know. She needed a name to go with the racing of her heart, the need to be close to him. None of it made sense. She needed something to make sense. He looked familiar. Her heart recognized him even if her mind didn't.

"Dylan." John grinned as he walked away. Joe was gone, but she had this feeling she couldn't understand that, somehow, she knew that she'd love again. The thought saddened her in the same way that made her smile.

"It's a great party," a man she didn't know said as he approached to stand beside her.

"It always is." She smiled and took another sip from her flute.

"I'm about to be one of the most requested attorneys in town. I'm about to deliver a Christmas present that will make my client's entire year," the man said while gesturing to where Dylan and a group of people stood around talking.

"Oh?" she asked.

"He asked for me to perform a miracle, and I have. I found the loophole he needs to give him back his family home."

Her heart dropped into her stomach as memories came rushing back as though someone had opened the floodgates. She grabbed the man's arm before she fell. She remembered Dylan, how he'd stormed into her house and into her life. He'd lived with her, and he'd told her his secrets, all of them...but this one.

"Miss, are you okay?" the attorney asked.

"Yes," she answered, but her words came out a whisper. "Who's your client?" In her heart, she already knew the answer.

"Dylan Sawyer."

She closed her eyes and let her head fall forward when her fear hit her between the eyes. "I didn't realize he was looking for a way to get it back."

"Yep, since the day he arrived. I'm about to go deliver the good news." He held up an envelope in his hand. "When they settled the estate, the wrong person got served, and now I can prove it. It's just the angle he needs to fight the current owner, Ms. Lily—"

"Bennett," she answered for him and turned to smile. His eyes bulged in surprise, and she slid the envelope from his fingers. "That would be me. Why don't I go share the great news?"

Lily set her flute down on a passing tray as she headed in Dylan's direction. Different scenarios filtered through her mind. He'd wanted the house back since day one. She'd known that when she agreed to give him first option to buy. She also knew he loved her. He may have started down this road, but somewhere along the way he veered. She trusted him with more than the fate of her house, she trusted him with her heart.

She held his gaze, and all of the love she'd felt for him warmed her chest and crept into her cheeks. She may have returned his heart, but he owned hers. She smiled as she approached, excusing herself and him as she took him by the arm and whisked him away.

"Lily?"

"Oh, how sweet." She glanced up at him. "You do remember my name."

"I wasn't the one that forgot," he replied.

Lily pulled Dylan into the formal dining room where they could have their talk in private, away from prying eyes.

She turned to face him. "Your attorney found a loophole to get you the house back."

"You remember me? You remember us?" His eyes lit up like a kid on Christmas morning. He took the envelope and tossed in on the table and pulled her into his arms. "Screw the house. It doesn't matter. I've missed you. God, how I've missed you."

He pressed his lips to hers as he clutched her close. He whispered against her lips. "I thought I'd lost you."

She relaxed into his embrace and felt as though she was finally home. Her mind and her heart both knew she was right where she belonged.

She couldn't contain the smile from her lips as she broke the kiss. "I found your Heart."

"You are my heart and my soul." Dylan pulled a box out of his tuxedo pocket and opened it. "Marry me, Lily, and be my wife."

Lily gazed down at the platinum ring with a ruby heart positioned on top, surrounded by a circle of tiny diamonds.

"Is that...?"

Dylan grinned. "Yes. The only part of the Ruby I kept. The rest I donated to the children's home."

Lily's heart felt full. Some people never experience a full heart, and others only for one person, but Lily knew how blessed she was. For the second time in her life, she was exactly where she was supposed to be and with the man who loved her. Lily nodded as unshed tears filled her eyes. "Yes. I'll marry you."

He pulled her near and kissed her like a man on the verge of starvation. He took the ring out of the box and slid it on her finger. "We should tell the others."

"There's no need." She pointed to the security cameras around the room, the red lights blinking and recording the entire event.

She held her hand up to the camera, showing off her new ring, and smiled.

****

A year later, with the wedding behind them, Lily gazed into the fireplace listening to the embers crack and pop as it warmed the room. She snuggled beneath the quilt that had been handed down from one generation to the next, each woman in the family owning and understanding that the Heart wasn't just a gem of gregarious proportions, but that it also represented the love that was felt for the Sawyer men.

"Penny for your thoughts?" Dylan asked as he wrapped his arms around his wife and pulled her into his side.

"I understand now."

"Oh?" he asked while rubbing lazy circles on her arm.

"The importance and meaning behind the quilt." She grinned and looked up at him. "It wasn't just a map."

"Sure it was," he teased.

She got on her knees and climbed over him, straddling his thighs like the first time they'd made love.

"It's a reminder to love each other." Lily smiled. "One day we'll pass it down to our children."

Dylan chuckled as he rubbed her back. "If it lasts that long." He rubbed at the fabric between his fingers. "This old thing has been around for several generations."

"Good thing I know how to sew," she teased. "We might need it sooner than you think."

Dylan's eyes bulged, and his fingers stilled. "Lily...."

She lifted her hand and placed it on her flat belly. "Say hello to your son. I only pray he gets the call like you and me and the ones before us." Lily raised her hand and admired the platinum wedding band that complemented her engagement ring. "We still have a piece of the heart. It's possible."

"Anything's possible, baby." He leaned forward and kissed her lips. "I've waited my whole life to love you, and you were most definitely worth the wait."

The End.

I hope you enjoyed reading the Bennett Series as much as I've enjoyed writing their stories. Please keep reading if you'd like to start my new Sophie Series. Here's a sample of the first book, Lifting the Veil that can be found on Amazon.

Chapter 1

"Freak Fest has officially begun," Sophie Masterson whispered, to her best friend, while cautiously shifting her steps farther away from the shirtless man staring at her. His entire chest and face were painted in some type of white flour base accentuating the bright purple color of his eyes.

"Can you believe we're in Salem on Halloween night, Sophie? We're here.

We're actually here." Amber's tone vibrated with excitement.

Salem was the exact opposite of Easton, the small town where Sophie grew up and called home.

Tourists traversed in and out of the shops along the cobblestoned streets. Every window they passed contained advertisements for readings, boasting their psychics were the best in town. Religious preachers lined the street corners, with their obedient followers, holding up signs damning everyone to hell for partaking in the activities. Women and men dressed up as witches and warlocks passed by. The eerie town appeared creepier as they walked farther into the activities. This was Sophie's first and last experience, if her vote counted.

The sun dipped and disappeared behind the brick buildings as the sky turned to night. The full moon predicted for this evening was barely visible, peeking from behind the cloud-covered sky. A man perched on the street corner blew his saxophone to the tune of a death march. The town went all out to entice the spiritual hungry tourists and those just out for a good time. Sophie was neither.

A hand snaked out, clutching Sophie's arm and dragging her to a stop. A woman wearing a long black dress grasped her painfully tight. Her red-painted fingernails were digging a groove into Sophie's skin. Her stomach churned with frustration while trying to pry the woman's fingers loose. "Get off me."

"You're a sleeper," the crazy lady hissed through blood-red painted lips that matched the color of her nails. "Your time is coming soon."

Her gray, hypnotic eyes swirled to life, renewing Sophie's vigor to break free. "You're on crack, lady."

"Back off!" Amber glared at the old woman while frantically trying to pry away the fingernails embedded in Sophie's arm. Amber grabbed the woman's index finger and pulled it back in an unnatural angle, almost breaking the bone.

Sophie wrenched her arm free. Fresh scratch marks marred her skin as blood droplets formed on the surface. Cupping the injured arm to her chest, Sophie backed away.

"Keep your creepy hands to yourself," Amber scolded. "Personal space, people. Personal space."

Sophie pulled a tissue out of her purse and dabbed at the new marks.

"Are you okay?"

"Yeah, I'll be fine. She just caught me off guard."

Unease shivered down Sophie's spine. These people were crazy, one hundred percent insane. Sophie swallowed around the coal-sized lump in her throat while silently reminding herself this would be her last trip, no matter how much Amber begged to come again.

Amber glanced behind them while tugging on Sophie to keep walking. "Freak incident. I'm sure the rest of the people aren't all grabby. We're still going to have a good time, if I have to beat every single one of them off of you, damn it. They are not raining on my parade."

That was Amber, feisty with a bit of a wild side. She loved anything and everything weird and unexplainable. It wasn't uncommon for her to scan the night skies for UFOs or trek through the forest in search of Bigfoot. Whatever hair-brained idea Amber came up with, she always managed to talk Sophie into tagging along. This trip was no different.

Partygoers and weirdoes lurked everywhere they turned, and they hadn't even made it inside the festival doors.

"Remind me again why I let you talk me into this."

"Because we're going to have fun."

"Yeah... when does that start?"

"Look around, Soph, the fun has already started." Amber grinned. "Besides, it's your duty as my best friend to be there for me when I'm told when Mr. Right is going to make his appearance. He's overdue."

"Maybe he lost his map," Sophie joked, earning her a glare from her best friend.

A group of teenagers congregated around the front door, blocking the entrance to the psychic fair. Was that an omen of what lay waiting inside?

Amber shooed them with her hands, parting the crowd like the Red Sea. "Move aside, people. You're standing in the way of my destiny."

She opened the door and led the way down the twisting corridors in one of the creepiest buildings in town. Musk and mildew filled the air. Water stains covered the concrete floor.

"Are you sure this isn't hazardous to our health?"

"Who cares? Don't you want to know what the future holds?"

"Not unless you can assure me they're willing to tell me the lottery numbers, so I don't have to search for a job when we get back."

Amber rolled her eyes, following Sophie. Posted signs and arrows hung crooked on the bland white walls leading them through a labyrinth to where the festivities loomed. The creepy street outside might have given her the shivers, but that was nothing compared to the building they were in. At least outside she had space to run and escape, unlike in the small, dimly lit hallway winding to nowhere. The new location brought the ambiance of eerie to a whole new level. Her breathing turned labored and her heart beat erratically. The walls appeared to be shrinking around her. She took a deep breath, ignoring the possibility of spores entering her lungs as she tried to tamp down her claustrophobia attack. If the lights suddenly went off or scary music started playing, it was every man and woman for themselves. Sophie wasn't waiting around to see if these haunted halls came to life. Anxiety ate at her gut as they rounded each corner. A small irrational part of her mind feared a knife-wielding, life-sized version of Chucky would be waiting to attack.

They slowed down at the fair entrance and eased into the larger room. Sophie could read the mild disappointment in her friend's eyes. Her sails momentarily deflated at the size of the small gathering.

"I'm sorry, Amber. I know you were expecting more...flair and fun."

Amber shrugged. "It's fine."

Vendors were stationed along the walls of the big concrete room. The strong scent of a decade's-old potpourri assaulted her nose. The scent entered every pore of her body and into her mouth. It saturated her hair and clothing while making the room appear smoky. It was worse than the bingo hall she'd accompanied her grandma to; and that spoke volumes.

"What is that god-awful smell?" Sophie asked while covering her nose.

"Sage," the answer came from a tall, dark-haired man wearing more black eyeliner than both Sophie and Amber combined. He towered over her five-foot-seven-inch frame, making her feel small. He greeted them with a flyer before gesturing to his booth. "Feel free to look around and if you have any questions just ask. We're a friendly lot."

Sure they were. They probably hexed anyone unwilling to part with their cash. Her nerves were strung tight, her mind playing different scenarios while she followed Amber around the room. Tables occupied the middle of the room. Psychics wielding tarot cards worked their spreads on the metal surfaces, reading the eagerly awaiting men and women who sat in front of them. Her best friend stopped at one of the vendors' booths that featured a crystal ball. Amber picked up one of the blue stones next to it and held it up to the light, twisting and turning, watching the light dance off of the reflective surface.

"Don't do that. It's probably hexed," Sophie whispered, hoping not to be overheard.

"Lighten up, Soph. We're here to experience."

Yeah, experience what? Amber made her way around the rest of the room, Sophie hot on her heels, feeling awkward and out of place. Men and women watched, their gazes following Sophie around the room as if she was a creature they'd yet to encounter. They remained eerily silent in passing, just watching, as if waiting for her to sprout horns. Amber lingered at each table, taking her time touching and admiring most of everything she could have simply bought on the Internet for a better price. She was coming home with a hex. There was no doubt about it. Amber paused in front of a table with two women manning a cash box. A plastic frame stood near them, holding the flyer with the price sheet for the psychic readings.

Sophie scanned the prices and couldn't stop her mouth from parting and eyes from bulging. The prices were outrageous. She was in the wrong business. Her mind quickly wondered if any of the psychics or vendors might need a personal accountant. Maybe she could find employment among these ranks since she'd yet to find it anywhere else.

Amber signed the log and handed over some bills before returning to Sophie's side.

"I can't believe you're doing this."

Amber wrapped her arm around Sophie's and grinned. "You are too."

Sophie's mouth fell open. "The sage must be affecting your memory. I'm jobless. I don't have the money to blow on something like this. I'm lucky my brother offered to buy my ticket in the first place."

Amber smiled and winked while clicking her tongue, a sure sign she was up to no good. "I paid. You have no choice."

"That's crazy. I'm only here because you want this done. You shouldn't have done that."

"Consider it an early birthday present."

Amber unlinked her arm while they waited their turn near one of the booths.

She leaned into Sophie and whispered, "Why are all of these people staring at you?"

"I don't know. I thought I was being paranoid, but I'm not, am I?"

"It's your aura," a dark-haired woman, standing at the closest booth, explained. Her black shirt read, Charmed and Fabulous. She held out her hand. "I'm Theresa."

Theresa was a good solid name. Sophie expected something more exotic like Madame Serena, goddess of the stars, holder of light. Sophie brushed the thought aside and shook her hand. "What did you say about my aura?"

"It's violet and vibrant, unlike the muted colors we generally see. It's very unique. That's why they're staring. They can see the energy field that surrounds you."

Riiiight. The woman had looked normal until she said that she could see auras and energy fields. Seriously, who does that! Little black bottles lined her booth. Her flyer read, Flower Essences. Each one was designed and as unique as the woman who owned them. She picked up three and handed them to Sophie. "Take them daily and, by the next full moon, you should notice the difference. Some people notice the difference almost instantly."

"Why the full moon? Am I going to turn into a werewolf?" Sophie asked sarcastically.

Theresa's brows dipped and confusion riddled her face. "No. They'll just help you find that job you're searching for."

Theresa must have overheard her conversation. Sophie twisted the bottle to read the name. Rockstar. The contents were advertised to enhance more confidence and drive. The second was named Charmed, to be used for opening up psychic ability, and the third was Divine, for help meeting your guides and the archangels. That was the last thing that Sophie needed. She tried to hand them back. "I can't afford them."

"It's my gift to you." The charmed woman winked and cupped Sophie's fingers around the little bottles before handing

Sophie her card. "Call me if you have any questions, any questions at all."

"Uh...okay." Sophie glanced at Amber's excited face, and there was no way Sophie could continue arguing. She turned back to Theresa and smiled. "Thank you."

"Enjoy." She gestured to the empty table where the psychic readers patiently sat waiting. "It looks like they're ready for you."

Sophie stepped over to one of the empty tables and eased into the chair. The psychic sitting opposite looked to be about the same age of twenty-seven, give or take a year or two. Her blond hair hung down to her waist. Her one-inch long, French-manicured nails tapped lightly on the cards while the woman gave Sophie a gentle inviting smile.

"Go easy on me. I'm a virgin."

"No, you're not." The woman's laughter rang like music through the room.

"Well, this is my first time."

The psychic's eyes sparkled with intelligence and confidence as she set the tarot cards aside.

Sophie's gaze watched her every movement, looking for the earpiece or whatever gadget would be feeding her information.

"I'm not even going to need the cards for you." The woman rested her crossed arms on the table. "Your aura tells me enough."

"Oh?" Sophie questioned, wondering what bat-shit wisdom the woman was going to start preaching.

"You're a sleeper, a late bloomer to the awakening."

Sophie's stomach twisted in a knot. Sleeper, awakening, what in the heck was this woman going on about?

"What does that mean?"

"You have any headaches lately?"

Sophie shook her head.

"Heard any strange noises in your house, any ringing in your ears, any voices in your head?"

This woman was quickly losing ground. *This may take a while.* Sophie leaned back farther into her chair, getting comfortable.

"No...afraid not."

Sophie's confidence with this stranger telling her something useful continued to dwindle with each syllable.

"I see."

Apparently not. Sophie gave her a fake smile. Her mind scrambled, trying to recall if Amber might be eligible for a refund.

"Okay...well, it seems I get to be the bearer of good tidings."

"Good tidings? Mmm hmm."

"You have abilities. They are latent but will soon surface. The color of your aura suggests that the time is close."

Sophie crossed her arms over her chest. "Is that right?"

"I'm afraid so, hun." She grabbed the tarot cards, shuffled, and began to lay them out across the table but not in any particular pattern like on the tables around her. "Let's see what else is going on with you."

As if that wasn't enough. Ha. Sophie berated the woman in her mind.

"You're currently jobless, are you not?"

Sophie nodded, knowing the woman must have overheard Sophie and Amber's conversation. *Grab hold of what you know and work with it,* Sophie teased in her mind.

"You'll be working sooner than you think." She flipped a few more cards. "It seems that more than one job offer is going to come at the same time, so you'll have to choose."

Great...even if it was a load of bull.

"Okay."

She flipped three more cards and paused. Her smile slipped, her gaze intent. "That can't be," she whispered to herself.

Sophie waited and watched as the woman gathered the cards again and shuffled. She set them down in front of Sophie and asked her to cut the deck before she flipped the first three cards again.

The death card was kind of creepy looking, but she wouldn't have expected less while in Salem. The second was a guy with five of swords surrounding him, and the last card was an Ace with swords as well. The Ace had to be a good card, right?

The reader's face clouded with unease, her once-welcoming smile replaced with a frown.

Alarm bells rang in Sophie's mind. She sat forward in her chair. "What? What does that mean?"

The psychic glanced up, her gaze now serious. "The death card generally means transformation, which I assumed meant your abilities." She pointed down to the cards surrounding the death card. "These indicate conflict and raw power, possibly even something more sinister."

"I thought readings were supposed to be all love and light and airy. What the hell are you talking about with death and sinister?"

"They generally are, but yours... not so much. My guides are telling me that you will do great things with your gifts, once you accept them." She glanced back down at the cards. "But these are showing me other variables at play. You need to be careful." She leaned forward and grasped Sophie's hand. "You create your own destiny, not these cards. You have free will, and you need to remember that."

Sophie snatched her hand back as if she'd been burned and quickly rose, almost knocking the chair behind her over. Her heart hammered in her chest. The reader rose too and handed her a business card. "You're going to need guidance. Call me if I can help."

Like hell. Sophie took a deep, calming breath, remembering this stuff wasn't real.

"Thanks." She shoved the card into her pocket and moved to stand near the front door, waiting on Amber to get finished. Her mind was scrambling to reassure herself that this was a bunch of bull hockey. None of this was true. Just because someone claimed she could see Sophie's destiny in some stupid cards didn't mean that it was real. It wasn't possible.

Sophie stood around for ten agonizing minutes being stared at like a leper. The hair on her neck stood on end, every fiber in her screaming at her to leave the place.

Finally, and not a minute too soon, Amber bounced over, grinning from ear to ear. "Oh my god, mine was great."

"Tell me about it on the way out." Sophie grabbed Amber's hand and started ushering her back through the corridors at a quicker pace then when they'd arrived. Amber rambled on about her reading, her love life, career, and the money in her future the entire way. It wasn't until they were seated on the train that she came down from her high and asked the dreaded question Sophie could have predicted was coming next. *Ha...she could be psychic too.* She mentally laughed at herself.

"How was yours?"

Sophie shrugged. "I apparently have the same abilities as those quacks, and it's going to show up soon."

Amber's eyes bugged wide. "Oh my god...I can just call you now." Her brows dipped. "If that's okay."

"Sure...if it were true."

"You don't think it is?"

"Nope, I haven't had any headaches, no ringing in my ears, and no dead people talking to me."

"Hmm. Well, maybe it can still happen."

"Don't hold your breath."

She chuckled. "Did she say anything else? Is there a Mr. McDreamy coming into your life, anything positive?"

"She predicted I'll have my choice of job offers. I guess that's positive, if it comes true."

Amber smiled a big bright smile. "I knew it. Things are going to turn around for you."

Sophie leaned back into her seat and replayed the words back through her mind. If her friend wanted to think that Sophie's life contained all rainbows and roses, who was she to burst that bubble? Amber's head was firmly in the clouds where she lived, while Sophie's remained planted in reality. If any of this were to come true, there was no way she could explain any of it to her brother. He was ten years older than her and the head honcho at their small police department after all. He'd have her locked up or worse...committed.

ABOUT THE AUTHOR

Kate has lived in Florida for most of her entire life. She enjoys a quiet life with her husband, Michael and two kids.

Kate has pulled all-nighters finishing her favorite books and also writing them. She says she'll sleep when she's dead or when her muse stops singing off key.

She loves creating worlds full of suspense, secrets, hunky men, kick ass heroines, steamy sex and oh yeah the love of a lifetime. Not to mention an occasional ghost and other supernatural talents thrown into the mix.